Each month Harlequin publishes
12 new novels: six in the
"Harlequin Romance" series and six
in the "Harlequin Presents..." series.

 Each Harlequin novel is a beautiful
love story — inordinately interesting,
intriguingly informative, excitingly
entertaining — without the overtness or
violence so common in many forms of
entertainment today. Harlequin Books
take you to exciting, faraway places —
places where engrossing, believable
characters face real love situations.

 You will find yourself quickly drawn
into the story and will be reluctant to
put it down until the fascinating,
romantic plot is finally resolved.

 You will enjoy Harlequin Books,
just as millions of other women
like you have for years.

What readers say about Harlequin Books

"I can't imagine my reading life without Harlequin."
J. L.,* Sioux Falls, South Dakota

"I just read my first three Harlequins. It is Sunday today, otherwise I would go back to the bookstore to get some more."
E. S., Kingston, Ontario.

"I'm really hooked and I love it."
M.S., Richmond, Virginia

"Harlequins help me to escape from housework into a world of romance, adventure and travel "
J. R., Glastonbury, Connecticut

* Names available on request

VIOLET WINSPEAR

the honey is bitter

Harlequin Books

TORONTO・LONDON・NEW YORK・AMSTERDAM
SYDNEY・HAMBURG・PARIS・STOCKHOLM

Harlequin Presents edition published May 1973
ISBN 0-373-70506-9

Second printing May 1973
Third printing May 1973
Fourth printing August 1973
Fifth printing November 1973
Sixth printing July 1974
Seventh printing August 1974
Eighth printing March 1976
Ninth printing May 1976
Tenth printing August 1976
Eleventh printing September 1976
Twelfth printing November 1976
Thirteenth printing February 1977
Fourteenth printing May 1977
Fifteenth printing July 1977
Sixteenth printing November 1977
Seventeenth printing April 1978
Eighteenth printing September 1978
Nineteenth printing October 1978
Twentieth printing December 1978
Twenty-first printing February 1979
Twenty-second printing March 1979
Twenty-third printing June 1979
Twenty-fourth printing August 1979

Original hardcover edition published in 1967
by Mills & Boon Limited

CHAPTER ONE

HER wedding dress was made from yards of lovely Greek silk, her headdress was a tiny silver coronet from which cascaded a lace veil patterned with many tiny hearts. No one in the congregation guessed, as Domini came down the aisle on her bridegroom's arm, that she had married him out of fear rather than love.

They left for the Cornish coast an hour later, and took a taxi from the station to the small beachside villa which Paul Stephanos had rented for a week, before they flew on to Athens. He had always wanted to see something of the west coast, he told Domini, and now his chance had come.

Paul's Greek manservant and his wife Lita were already installed at the villa, and everything was looking cosy and welcoming. It had been a fairly warm spring day, but with the sinking of the sun a breeze had come in from the sea and Yannis had lit a fire in the lounge.

Entering this firelit room gave Domini the first warm feeling she had known all day. Paul threw off his topcoat and proceeded to examine the interior of the cocktail cabinet, where a couple of gold-capped bottles stood waiting to provide the honeymooners with a private toast. "Good, Yannis remembered our champagne!" There was a pleased, almost boyish note in the deep foreign voice.

Domini knelt warming her hands by the fire, in which driftwood burned and threw out little blue flames. Her honey-coloured hair fell in a shining wing down over her profile, hiding the look of terror, almost, that sprang into her eyes at Paul's remark. It would be like drinking hemlock, she told herself wildly.

5

"Let me help you off with your coat." Paul lifted her to her feet and his fingers were deft, unbuttoning her cream wool coat and slipping it off her shoulders.

She pushed her hands through her hair, while he regarded her with amused eyes. "Most women would be busily combing and powdering at the mirror after that long train journey," he said. "I begin to suspect that you are quite without any vanity—or is it a conceit in itself, Domini, your apparent disregard for the fact that you are beautiful?"

She heard him tiredly and faced him with a composure that was going rapidly to shreds. She felt cold to the heart of her, while her mind seemed to be running in all directions to escape from the thought that she was really here in Cornwall and married to *this* man.

"Paul, are you really going through with this—this marriage you've forced me into?" The words broke from her; she could hold them in no longer.

Coolly, deliberately he took out his cigarette case and held it towards her. She shook her head, watching a tiny confetti horseshoe fall from his dark sleeve as he lit a cigarette. "I gave you a choice, my dear," smoke drifted from his nostrils. "I did not force you to the altar at the point of a gun."

A choice? Domini shuddered at the word. Did he really believe that?

Her blue eyes were dark with fear and bewilderment as they scanned his face. They finally settled on the scar that jagged into his right temple; the scar alone seemed to make him human. That alone proved that he was at least physically vulnerable. "I-I can't believe that you're made of granite, Paul," she said. "But you act as though you are. As though it doesn't worry you in the slightest degree that you've invaded my life and snatched me away from all I love—just to be your toy! Do you think I can ever forgive you for that—ever like you for it?"

"You talk like a snatched Sabine woman, my dear." He flicked ash into the fire, and the smile in his tawny eyes was an enigmatic one. "I am well aware of how you regard me, but to be liked is a trivial emotion, and I have no time to spend on trivialities. I have few weaknesses, Domini, but one of them is a love of the unusual, the rare—you are a very rare creature, I think. You are lovely but unworldly, with a mystique about you that could be hiding anything—ice or flame."

He lifted his cigarette and drew deeply on it. "I wanted you," he said deliberately, "from the first moment we met at Fairdane."

He captured her gaze and held it forcibly. "The day I found out about those forgeries of your cousin's," he went on, "I drove down to Fairdane in a black fury, determined to tell your uncle what his wretched son had done—and you were there. You were still away at school the last time I was in England, but that particular day you had just come in from a walk on the heath and the wind had whipped your mouth to a rose and your eyes to blue gems. I looked at you, but I did not see a schoolgirl, and from that moment your cousin's indiscretion was a weapon in my hands.

"You flinch, Domini, but I was hoping not to use that weapon. I hoped you might—anyway, it became plain at the end that you merely regarded me as the tough Greek who employed your cousin as assistant-manager to one of the Stephanos shipping-line offices—"

There he paused, and a nerve jarred in Domini's throat as a piece of firewood broke in half and the resin hissed and flared.

"I wanted you, Domini," Paul's smile was strange, without humour. "At any price."

She shuddered, hating his brutal honesty, yet also aware that if he had talked about loving her, she would have been filled with contempt. Her glance ran wildly

over him, as it had that first day they had met at Fairdane, when instinct had swiftly warned her that he was
a threat to her peace with his pagan face, his smoky-
gold tiger's eyes, and his hair that was like the close-
curled fleece of a black ram.

Involuntarily she backed away from the power and
danger in his lounging body, there by the mantelpiece.
"I-I don't think I can go through with our marriage,
Paul," her voice shook, though she tried to keep it
steady. "You've forced me into a cruel, uncivilised
situation and you're without a scrap of feeling for me."

"Your own pride forced you to choose me in pre-
ference to seeing the name of Dane dragged through the
criminal courts," he pointed out. "And why should I
pity you, when I would sooner admire you for being
one of those who would suffer rack and flame rather
than have mud thrown at those you love?" And then he
flicked his half-smoked cigarette into the fire and stepped towards her. Again she backed away from him,
right to the edge of the big couch, slim and helpless in
his lean hands as they took hold of her.

"Come, I am not such a monster," he murmured, and
she saw the deep golden glow of his eyes between dense
black lashes. "I can be quite nice, especially to a lovely
thing like you. So lovely, so full of pride—and icy fire."

With sudden possessiveness he gathered her close to
him and laid his lips where her throat was gently hol-
lowed and delicately shaded by the white lace of her
blouse. His lips were warm, searching, and she felt a
tremor run through him as his face touched the softness
of her skin. Tears stung the corners of her eyes as he
took her lips. Tears for the girl she could never be again.
Tears for the bride he had bought.

His warm, chiselled mouth finally lifted from hers,
and she lay passive against his hard shoulder, gazing up
at him with the eyes of a child expectant of a punish-

8

ment she had not earned. His kiss had not moved her, but it had shown her how much he wanted her!

"My little *Anglitha,* have you stopped smiling for ever?" he asked quizzically. "Are you always going to look at me with such reproachful eyes?"

"What did you expect," she asked, "eyes full of tenderness?"

"I wonder how you would look, with eyes full of tenderness?" He ran a finger down the delicate curving of her cheekbone and let it linger at the corner of her mouth, flushed from his kiss and tremulous, as though it wouldn't take much more to make her cry. Suddenly his arms enclosed her with more gentleness. "I am not asking you to love me, Domini," he said, "but don't quite hate me."

"I despise you!" The words sprang fiercely to her lips, and she resented his nearness, the touch of his hands, and the fact that his face was the handsomest she had ever seen, despite that scar above his right eye. Handsome and ruthless!

"Ah, well," he said, and his lips brushed her temple, and he released her from his arms as tea things jingled on a tray and Yannis came into the room.

He brought the tray to a low table beside the couch and Domini sat down to pour out, her eyes and mouth alone showing colour in her face. Paul had taken the villa furnished, and she guessed from the look of the place that he must be paying a high rent for it. His money frightened her; it had turned him into a man who thought he could buy everything, a man who didn't know, or didn't care, that there were some things you could never buy—like the love and honour she had vowed that day to give him.

"I am pleased you remembered the champagne, Yannis," he said, as the manservant turned from making up the fire. "We will, of course, have it with our wed-

9

ding supper. No doubt Lita is preparing something really memorable for us, eh?"

Domini, glancing up, saw the rather grave-faced Greek break into a slight smile. He was a man of few words, though obviously devoted to his master, and after assuring his new young mistress that their wedding supper would be ready in an hour, he withdrew quietly from the room.

Domini handed Paul his cup and saucer. He sipped at the brew, and then said with a laugh: "I wonder if I shall ever get used to English tea?"

"Why didn't you order coffee?" she asked coldly.

"I know you prefer tea, my dear." He sat down on the arm of the couch and she had to force herself not to move away from him. The hot sweet tea brought a little life back into her cold body, but she wasn't grateful to Paul for providing it. She told herself she would hate the things he would give her, for each item would be displayed on his possession as the white gown today had been, and the veil, ivory with age, which had been sent all the way from his home on the island of Andelos in the Ionian Sea.

Without looking at him, she said: "Have you burned those forged cheques as you promised to?"

"Not yet."

And when she looked quickly up at him, he smiled faintly. "You might take it into your lovely head to run away from me, so those incriminating cheques are staying unburned—until tomorrow."

She flushed painfully, understanding all too clearly what he meant. "Y-you promise to burn them tomorrow?" She spoke almost inaudibly, while her fair skin seemed to retain her painful blush for at least a minute.

"I shall burn them in your presence," he assured her.

A few minutes later they went upstairs to dress for dinner. Their suite was decorated in several shades of lilac and there was a bathroom attached to each bedroom. Domini dallied in her bath until she heard the adjoining door close and she knew Paul had bathed and dressed and gone downstairs. Then she wrapped herself in a big lilac-coloured towel and went into her bedroom. As she approached the dressing-table her glance fell on a jeweller's box that had not been there when she had gone in to bath. She gazed at it as though at something that could turn on her and bite. Paul had brought it in, and she toyed with the idea of placing it, unopened, on his dressing-table. But the next moment, with a shiver, she realised that he would only force her to wear whatever was in the box.

She reluctantly lifted the lid and found on a bed of oyster silk an exquisite heart-shaped pearl brooch, with several rubies falling like tears of blood from the indentation of the heart. There were earclips to match.

Domini stared at the set, which seemed to mock her with its symbolic beauty. Then she dragged the brooch from its bed and threw it blindly across the room. Angry tears choked her and she lay on her bed crying her heart out, hot, bitter tears unlike any she had ever shed before in her life at Fairdane. She had loved the place, and even coping with a limited housekeeping budget had never worried her.

She had been her own mistress, the adored niece of Martin Dane, who had treated her like a daughter ever since she had come to him as a baby, her parents having drowned in a boating accident . . .

Then, in the midst of her tears, she sat up. She pushed the tousled hair back from her wet cheeks and stared, heart leaping, at the adjoining bedroom door. Paul had said he would destroy those cheques tomorrow, therefore he must have them here at the villa—in his room! She scrambled off her bed, her tears forgotten as she made for his door. If she found the cheques she could

11

destroy them herself and be free of Paul Stephanos! Her heart bounded at the thought; the villa was fairly close to Looe and she would certainly be able to get a room there for the night.

Her bath-towel was slipping and she hastily adjusted it like a sarong, then she turned the handle of Paul's door and switched on the light. There were masculine toilet articles on the dressing-table, and his dark silk pyjamas and robe lay across the foot of the bed. The smoke of a cheroot lingered in the room and for a moment its sharp tang made Domini feel panicky. Then she crushed down her panic and advanced to the cupboard where his suitcases had probably been put away.

Her heart was hammering. She hadn't dared to hope that there might be a way of escaping from Paul and of winning back the independence she had always prized so much. It was true that four years ago, when she was seventeen, she had come close to falling in love with a young artist who had drifted into the seaside town where her boarding-school had been situated, but it had been a gay, innocent, fleeting romance. Barry had gone out of her life as he had come into it, and she hadn't heard from him since.

She opened the door of Paul's cupboard, and gave a nervous jump as her reflection sprang at her from the mirror inside the door. The burning imploration of her own eyes frightened her and she thrust the door back against the wall so that she could no longer see herself. The sleeve of a tweed jacket brushed her cheek as she bent forward to lift out the coachhide cases, and she pushed at the sleeve as though it was an arm reaching out to take hold of her.

Downstairs in the lounge Paul stood with a black-clad shoulder against the frame of one of the long windows, his gaze on the strip of beach that stretched away from the villa steps to the sea. The wind was getting up and foam-laced breakers were crashing over the rocks at the edge of the beach. The breakers shone, reflecting the light of the moon each time it drifted out from the clouds. The thunder of the sea could be heard plainly, and Paul touched a hand to his right temple, as though that pounding had an echo behind his scar. He dropped his hand as someone came into the room.

"Excuse me, sir," Yannis spoke in Greek, "there is a long-distance telephone call for Madame."

"For my wife?" Paul stepped out from the shadows near the window and there was a frown on his face. "I will take the call, Yannis," he said, and he strode out into the hall. He lifted the telephone receiver and gave his name. Immediately the voice of Martin Dane came on the line, and it shook with agitation.

"Paul, I must speak to Domini right away," he said. "Please bring her to the phone. It's imperative."

"What the devil has happened?" Paul's hand clenched on the telephone cord.

"My son—Douglas. He has told me about that money he took from you—those cheques he forged in your name." There was a pause, as though even yet Martin Dane could hardly believe that his son would do such a thing. "Paul, my son felt he had to tell me—for Domini's sake. He believes she has married you—*sold herself,* in fact, to save our wretched pride."

"Sold herself—to me?" The words cracked into the receiver. "What an archaic idea, Mr. Dane! It smacks of the Middle Ages."

"I *know* Domini, what she's capable of doing for those she loves." A fierceness came into her uncle's voice. "I also know that my niece could never love *you,* Stephanos. You're not her sort. You come from another world—are you still listening? Then I insist that you bring Domini to the phone so I can speak to her."

Paul stood silent, his face carved and harsh as he gazed at the wall-etching above the telephone table. His tiger-gold eyes were glinting dangerously. "I am aware that I come from another land, Mr. Dane, and that I speak English with a foreign accent," then accentuating it, he added: "But none of that alters the fact that your lady niece is now my wife."

"The marriage can be annulled," Martin Dane said triumphantly.

"On what grounds?" Paul enquired politely.

"Non-consummation. That is the law."

"It might be the law, but it is also a fact that Domini and I have been alone here for a couple of hours. She is very desirable, Mr. Dane, and I am not an English gentleman."

The pause at the other end of the line was pregnant, and Paul gave a brief, unamused smile. Martin Dane was very much an English gentleman who lived his life by set rules. "Stephanos," the edge of his very English voice was torn and ragged, "let Domini go. You don't love her. You only want a lovely woman to dress up as your symbol of success in this jungle of a world. Money, glitter, they aren't important to Domini."

"But being able to hold up her head so she can look people squarely in the eye is important to her, Mr. Dane." Paul retorted. "Could any of you do that again, if I sent Douglas to prison?"

"Will you be able to hold up *your* head," Martin Dane said harshly "knowing all the time that you've forced Domini to become your wife? Why, she must be hating you!"

"I am a strange man," said Paul. "I would sooner be married to a woman who honestly hates me than to one who dishonestly loves me." With these words he placed the receiver on the cradle to break the telephone connection, then he lifted it again and laid it on its side on the table. It purred emptily as he crossed the small hall to the dining-room where Yannis was putting the finishing touches to the table. Paul told him that he had left the telephone off the cradle and that he wanted it to stay that way. Yannis did not question the order. He was a Greek, and Paul was master in his house.

"The table looks very festive." Paul fingered the velvety petals of the deep crimson roses in the vase between his place and Domini's. Tapering amber candles stood ready to be lighted.

"I shall be serving dinner in just ten minutes, sir," Yannis informed him.

"Then I had better go and fetch my wife. What a devil of a time women take to dress, eh?"

Yannis smiled, and watched with dark eyes as Paul strode out of the room. He too, touched the red roses and his sigh stirred the candle flames as they bloomed under the match he applied to them.

Paul bounded up the stairs and walked along the landing to the door of Domini's room. He tapped upon it. There was no answer, so he turned the handle and entered the room . . . his glance going at once to the door standing ajar between their rooms. He frowned and the thick bedroom carpet silenced his footfalls as he crossed over to that open door.

"What do you think you are doing?"

The question lashed out behind Domini, who had all the drawers of the tallboy and the dressing-table wide open, while his shirts, underclothing and ties were strewn all over the bed. She had ransacked the room very thoroughly and at the moment was sorting through the contents of the briefcase he had brought to the villa. It fell from her hands as she swung round, startled, to face Paul, and his business papers rained in confusion to the floor.

They stood staring at one another, and the mirthless

15

coldness of her husband's eyes chilled Domini from head to foot. He came across to her with long, hard steps, and his hands caught at her bare shoulders. The lilac towel was still draped around her like a sarong and she stumbled over the trailing end of it as Paul jerked her to him.

"What are you looking for, those cheques of your cousin's?" His mouth curled; a dark scroll of hair lay against the lividity of his scar. "My lovely, brainless idiot, do you really think I would be fool enough to keep them here, where you might get your hands on them? They are safely locked in a safety deposit box in a Looe bank. I brought them with me when I came to see about renting the villa."

CHAPTER TWO

THE cheques were safe at a bank in Looe!

With these words he quenched the spark of hope in Domini's heart, and she stood there without feeling the bruising anger of his hands. She might have guessed that he would not leave a loophole through which she could escape. He had paid too high a price for her, and he had not yet collected his due.

She stood there while his glance travelled over her, taking in the marks of tears on her pale cheeks, the way her wild-honey hair curled damply at the edges from her bath and contrasted with the milky skin of her neck and shoulders. A tiny pulse flickered beside Paul's mouth and its minute, hurrying life caught Domini's attention. Then her lashes swept down over her eyes as Paul lifted her into his arms with easy strength and carried her into her own room. He did not set her down immediately, but stood gazing down at her face. "How a look of simplicity can conceal a maze of complexities," he murmured. "You must dislike me very much, my little piece of femininity, to dare the devil in me by scattering my belongings all over my bedroom. You deserve a spanking for that."

"I-I'll tidy them up," she offered, lips quivering but chin tilted.

"You will get dressed," he said, and as he set her upon her feet she heard him catch his breath on a quiet laugh. "Domini, never try to run away from me. I shall always catch up with you and I shall hold you as long as it—pleases me."

The threat seemed to leap from his fingertips into her very bones as his hands gripped her. Then he let her go,

17

went into his room and quietly closed the door behind him.

He had gone in to refold his clothing and to rearrange the business papers she had dropped to the floor as though they were so much litter. He had succeeded in making her feel ashamed, and it was added fuel to the resentment burning within her as she started to dress.

It shimmered, that dress, fashioned of deep blue lace over white organza, a wedding gift from a friend who ran a gown shop in the West End of London. It was exquisitely styled, and Domini knew in her shrinking heart that fear of Paul made her put it on for her wedding supper with him. Her ransacking of his room had deeply angered him, and only by looking fragile in blue and white did she feel she could protect herself against the anger that might make him a terrible lover.

The ruby and pearl earclips still reposed in the box on the dressing-table, but when she finally located the brooch in a corner by the bed she found she couldn't pin it on. She couldn't wear the taunting, lovely thing, *not tonight,* and she clipped on instead the string of pearls she had worn with her wedding gown. They had belonged to her mother, and they seemed to give her a little courage.

She sprayed on *Vers Toi* perfume, then gazed for a long moment into her own unhappy eyes, face to face with the alarming burden she had taken on in marrying a man to save her family's pride. There would be none of the closeness and subtle communication of a true marriage. None of the joy, or the tender understanding.

With her nerves quivering like roots plucked out of protective soil, Domini made her way out of her room, on her way to a wedding supper that would seem like a victim's mock-merry meal. Paul caught her up as she reached the head of the staircase. She shot a side glance up at him, to see whether he was still furious with her, and his smile mocked the apprehension she couldn't hide. She felt his arm encircle her waist as they went downstairs together, and she endured its intimacy with a quick-beating heart. "You look like a moon-maiden in your blue and white gown," he said. "I almost feel that you will vanish behind a cloud quite suddenly and leave me all alone."

She glanced at him curiously as they entered the dining-room, and for the first time she wondered if he had married her for her company as much as her looks.

In evening wear he was more overwhelming than ever, she decided. His dark, Grecian looks were thrown into prominence rather than tempered down by the silk shirt and the black dinner-jacket. She wasn't a small girl, but his height made her feel one, and suddenly she was sensing that lonely aura some people carry about with them. Wealthy, good-looking in his own formidable way, this man was yet a lonely one—a lonely enigma whom she had married today, and whose wife she would become tonight!

Domini had not touched a morsel of food all day, and she was suddenly hungry as Yannis set an oyster cock-tail in front of her. "Mmm, this looks delicious," she said, and she gave him her sweet, flashing smile. It was a smile she had never given Paul, and she was unaware that he was looking at her as he stood opening the iced bottle of champagne. The cork popped loudly and the golden liquid bubbled down the side of the bottle. Paul dipped a finger in the champagne and dabbed a little behind Domini's ears, smiling quizzically at the tensing of her slender body. "Just for luck, Domini," he said half-mockingly, tipping the champagne bottle and fil-ling her wine glass.

He seated himself opposite her at the table and filled

his own glass. Then he raised it and murmured a toast in Greek.

Domini had started on her oyster cocktail. "May I know what you said?" she asked, without looking up at him.

"I merely said that in all the wedding cake, hope is the sweetest plum," he drawled.

Then she did look up and saw the candle flames move their shadows across his high cheekbones and his scarred temple. "It is a pity we could not have got to know each other better," he said. "To have had the dining, dancing and driving trysts which might have helped you to be—less shy with me. But that could not be helped. I had some important private business here in England which has taken up most of my time. It was this business that brought me here so unexpectedly."

She felt a chilliness steal over her, for his unexpected arrival in England had woven the first strands of the web she was now entrapped in. There had been no time for Douglas to recoup his gambling losses and so make good the substantial sum of money he had stolen from his employer. And she had not had the heart to see her cousin—weak but charming—go to prison for his folly. She could only hope that he had learned his lesson at her expense.

Roast lamb was brought in with rowan jelly, and then they had a liqueur soufflé that melted on the tongue. Yannis' wife served coffee in the lounge. She was a swarthy, intensely reserved woman with Romany blood in her veins. She handed Domini a small gift, which gave the girl so much genuine delight that for the moment she forgot that she wasn't a bride of love, as Lita and her husband thought. The wedding gift was a little chrome and glass basket filled with marzipan apples. "It's so pretty and unusual," Domini smiled. "Oh, how nice of you both!"

There was a grave, searching smile in Lita's eyes as they travelled over the upraised loveliness of Domini's young face. In the candleglow her face was delicately moulded, her eyes as deeply blue as the sapphire swirled in diamonds on her left hand. The wings of her wild-honey hair fell softly to her pale, bared shoulders.

"May joy be with you," Lita said. "And may you be blessed with a *chavo*."

An intense silence fell on the room as the door closed on Lita's dark-clad figure, then Domini could not keep her eyes from Paul's face. Her face was suddenly wiped free of pleasure, and her blue eyes were tormented. "What is a *chavo*?" she whispered.

"A boy child," Paul said quietly, the scar at his temple livid as fear leapt into her eyes before she could veil it. She bent quickly over the coffee tray and filled the little cups with the dark, aromatic Turkish coffee which Lita had made. When she handed Paul his cup her face was again composed into an expressionless mask.

They drank several cups of coffee, then Paul poured out some fragrant old brandy as a *chasse*. But Domini left hers untouched on the couchside table while she wandered restlessly about the room, looking at the paintings, picking up ornaments and putting them down again. At last she stood by the damask curtains at the long windows.

Throughout dinner she had maintained a certain measure of calm, but now it had faded and taken with it her transient interest in the island of Andelos, about which Paul had talked. His alien gestures had even fascinated her a little as he described the unspoilt charm of the island, and told her about his home high on a headland above a wild stretch of private beach. The house on the eagle's crag, the islanders called it.

"Let me go, Paul!" she spoke suddenly in a tortured

voice. "Let me go if you have any heart at all. You know I don't love you . . ." there her breath caught in her throat and one hand clenched the curtain as Paul rose from the couch and came across the room towards her. She saw all the leashed power in him, the tiger-like grace, and the autocracy that surely crushed all obstacles that barred his way to what he wanted.

She stood framed by the ivory-silk curtain, drawn back against it as though defying him to touch her. "And what am I supposed to do if I let you go?" he asked. "Do you expect me to burn those cheques just the same, and be satisfied with nothing but the ashes?"

"What can our marriage bring but the taste of ashes?" Desperation was a dry, bright glitter in her eyes as they dwelt on his face. The face of Apollo, dark and strange, every feature stamped with the unyielding Greek iron in him. "Force me to stay with you, Paul, and I shall hate you," she warned.

"Hatred and love are akin, my little Sabine," and as he spoke he laughed softly. "They are both blind emotions."

"There is no love between us." Her eyes flashed and rejected the very thought. "There never could be."

"Ah, but you speak about romantic love." He came a step closer and his hands rested warm at either side of her face, he held them there as she tensed, and searched her eyes. "What other love could you know about but the kind you read in the books of romance? What other love has been offered you but that of shy young Galahads with stumbling tongues?"

Her pulse raced when he said that, and she thought of Barry. Barry had fluttered her heart and made her wonder about love and its secrets.

"No man has ever told you that you have blue-into-purple eyes," Paul murmured. "They are like southern skies, with at the moment all the stars in hiding." He

22

bent his dark head and laid his lips in the soft join between her neck and shoulder. "You must understand, my Domini, that when I make a deal with anyone, I abide by my side of the bargain and I see to it that the other party abides by his."

"But that's business," she whispered, shocked. "This is our lives, our happiness. Paul, are you such a cynic that you don't believe in happiness? Are you so hard that you can't be hurt?"

"I cannot be hurt by what other people think of me," his voice had slightly hardened. "I am Greek and it is my own self-disapproval I must live with. Be that as it may, we made a bargain, Domini, and we sealed it in church this morning. You are my wife—and I am not letting you go."

And she could see that he meant every word. It was written all over his face, merciless, handsome face, with little flames beginning to leap in his tawny eyes as they travelled over her. Fear was a coiled spring inside her, quite suddenly it snapped and she wrenched out of his arms, twisted out of the long windows behind her and sped madly to the steps that led down to the beach.

The cold sea wind whipped through the lace and silk of her dress as she stumbled through the sand in her high heels. Overhead the moon floated behind a cloud and as deep shadow fell down about Domini, she cast a frightened glance over her shoulder. Paul was pursuing her like some avenging night-god . . . in the shifting light of the moon his face seemed satanic.

So strangely desperate was she to get away from him that she didn't realise how close she was to the water, and the rocks at the edge of the beach. The breakers were thundering in, great dark glistening wings of water, and Domini gave a cry as in her high-heeled slippers she suddenly stumbled over a rock and felt a great wave break over her. It lifted her and like a sand-limbed doll she was taken and carried out. The cold shock of the water took her breath, blocked her nostrils, and as she tumbled helplessly in the mill of the sea there was a roaring in her brain and ears.

"Domini!" a voice cried out, and her name was followed by a Greek word that was lost in the rage of the waves.

The storm clouds above the beach broke asunder as Paul dragged off his shoes and plunged into the foaming water. Lightning ripped as he swam strongly towards the pathetic uplift of one of his wife's slender arms, and he saw the pallor and desperation of her face in yet another flicker of harsh white lightning. A moment later his arms enclosed her in the water and she clung wildly, mindlessly to him, as to a life-spar. He held her head above the water and as her senses cleared a little, she realised who he was—Paul, her husband, into whose keep she gave her frightened body without another murmur.

He held her and fought his way back to the beach with her. He trudged up the sandy slopes, water streaming from his black evening suit, his arms tight about Domini, a shivering bundle of cold and fright, whose blue and white gown clung drenched and ruined on her body. Sand churned beneath Paul's urgent strides, then he was mounting the side steps of the villa and swinging into the lounge through the long windows.

Domini stirred in his arms, coughed a little, and trembled. When Paul glanced down at her, water spattered from his black hair on to her face, and her blue eyes shot wide open. Her lips moved, soundlessly, forming his name, and he said gently enough: "It is all right, my foolish child. You are safe now."

He made swiftly for the fireplace and uncaring of the water that streamed from both of them he laid her on the oyster-white couch and rang the bell insistently

24

for Yannis. When Yannis hurried into the room, Paul was on his knees beside the couch and holding a tot of neat whisky to Domini's chattering teeth. She sipped and gave a cough at the raw bite of the spirit, and saw the grave mask slip off Yannis's face as he gaped at her and Paul. "We took a stroll along the beach and my wife fell into the water," Paul said, in a crisp, dry voice. "Yannis, tell Lita I want hot-water bottles put into my wife's bed right away, also a hot bath run for her. And bring that thick bath-robe of mine down here. Hurry, now!"

Yannis ran all the way to the kitchen and in rapid Greek he explained to Lita what had happened. Her sharp, dark eyes flicked his face. "That is not good, Yannis, that such an accident should happen," she said. "They say that if you sing before breakfast you will cry before the night is over."

"What are you talking about, woman?" Yannis stared at her as she turned on the tap and filled a big kettle with water.

"Was *he* not singing before breakfast this morning?" Lita shook her head and frowned. "And for a bride and her husband to be walking on the beach with a storm coming on is curious."

"You think they had a quarrel—already?" Yannis exclaimed.

"I think you had better hurry and get that robe for him," his wife rejoined. "Hurry, or he will be shouting down the house."

After Yannis had fetched and delivered the robe, Paul said to Domini; "I am going to get you out of these sopping clothes—don't fight me or you will make yourself more exhausted than you are already."

She was exhausted, physically and mentally, and she shivered like a half-drowned kitten as Paul stripped off her ruined dress and underwear, his gaze quite impersonal now, his touch almost paternal as he enfolded her in the warm roughness of his bathrobe.

His solicitude was strangely comforting, and it seemed close to impossible that his manner had been so demanding such a short while ago. As he lifted her from the couch she let her arm encircle his neck and stay there as he carried her from the lounge and up the stairs to the lilac suite, where he handed her over to Lita.

"Ensure that my wife has a good warm soak," he requested, "then put her to bed and give her a hot milk drink—plain milk will be best. A malt drink will not settle too well on whisky."

Lita inclined her head, and did not miss the faintly derisive way he smiled as he bade his bride goodnight.

"Goodnight, Paul." Domini looked a sorry, waif-like figure in the trailing folds of his bathrobe, with her damp hair clinging to her neck. "I-I'm sorry for running out into the storm and getting us both into such a state."

"I am sorry also," he drawled, significantly. "Anyway, forget about it and have a good sleep. I will see you in the morning."

He strode into his own room, closing the door very firmly behind him and flicking the wet hair back off his forehead. A few minutes later Yannis joined him. "I have run a hot bath for you, sir," he said diffidently.

"What do you say, Yannis?" Paul glanced up from a moody gaze at the carpet.

"You are wet through, sir." Yannis tried not to look as though he was fussing, for Paul did not like a lot of fuss. "A bath is ready for you."

"Thank you, Yannis." Paul smiled briefly and lightly pressed his manservant's arm as he walked past him into the bathroom.

Domini fell into a dreamless sleep almost as soon as she finished her milk and turned out the bedside light. It was slumber that lasted about an hour, then sud-

26

denly it was no longer dreamless. She was running along a cold seashore, and she could hear the thunder of the waves and feel the sand dragging at the heels of her slippers. The moon watched her from behind a cloud like a staring face, and something was chasing her. She cast a quick glance over her shoulder and saw that it was a great cat, making absolutely no sound as it pursued her, its eyes glowing golden and fearful. A sob of terror broke from her. She was sure that if the beast caught her, it would rend her to pieces.

It drew closer, closer all the time, silent and swift, and just as it prepared to spring upon her — she screamed.

"Domini, child, whatever is the matter?" The voice woke her, the nightmare fled away, and she found that the bedside lamp was on and Paul was bending over her, holding her shoulders with warm, steadying hands. "My good girl," with irony and anxiety, "do you make a habit of screaming in your sleep?"

"D-did I scream?" She blinked at him in the lilac glow of the lamp, vaguely noticing that there were sleep-ruffled scrolls of black hair on his forehead, and that the dark silk coat of his pyjamas had come open, revealing a triangle of dark hair on his broad chest. "What's the time?" she asked. "Is it nearly morning?"

"It is just past midnight," his white teeth showed as he gave a droll smile, "and I only hope that Yannis and his wife did not hear that scream of yours."

His words vaguely jolted her heart, and yet she found herself smiling back at him. "I think I was having a nightmare," she murmured. "How strange. I haven't had one of those since I was a child."

Paul stared down at her for a moment, then he seated himself on the side of her bed and in a voice like rough velvet he said to her: "Was it a nightmare about me? But, Domini, I would never hurt you, don't you know

27

that? Can't you feel it?" He took her hand and brought it near his heart and pressed it there. The lamp played its muted lilac light over the strong bonestructure of his face, and there in his face Domini saw again the loneliness she had glimpsed earlier that evening.

She lay passive, looking at him with her great blue eyes, seeing a stranger who was also her husband. On the hand that he held to his strange, foreign, complex heart, there was the gold band that proclaimed his rights to her person and her life, yet it was not entirely in surrender to his lawful claims that she let herself be taken into his arms.

CHAPTER THREE

WHEN Domini awoke, bright morning light was spilling through the long lace curtains of her bedroom, but for several moments she was unable to make out where she was.

Her bemused eyes stole round the lovely lilac room and settled on the tea-service on the table beside her bed. She stared at the indentation which a head had left in the pillow beside her, and in a flash everything came back to her. She was married to Paul Stephanos, the handsome, enigmatic Greek shipping-line owner from whom her cousin Douglas had stolen a frightening sum of money. Her hands could still feel the smooth, steely hardness of Paul's broad shoulders, her mind still held the strange little Greek words he had whispered against her throat in passion last night. She remembered that she had fallen asleep in his arms.

She sat up and poured herself a cup of tea. She sipped at it with a smile on her lips, relaxed, curled slim and warm against her pillows, the ring on her left hand glinting with promise she hardly dared to think about.

After finishing her tea, she got up and bathed, and then dressed herself in a white silk blouse with magyar sleeves, and a pair of slim-legged slacks.

After combing her hair she clipped it back in blue slides, and noticed in the mirror the new look in her eyes—the deep, secret look of knowledge. A smile tilted the corners of her mouth, she put back her head and saw the creamy length of the throat Paul had kissed. Each vein, each curve, each pool had known his lips, and though she might yet fear him in the deeper recesses of her heart, his possession last night had not frightened her. She saw a flush steal into her cheeks, and turned quickly away from her own eyes.

When she entered the dining-room, Paul was at the table immersed in the morning paper and a chunky sweater. He put his head round the paper and smiled at her "Good morning, Madame Stephanos," he said.

"Good morning, Paul." She stood rather shyly at the side-table, trying to make up her mind whether to have fried eggs and bacon, or scrambled eggs and kidneys. She decided on the latter and after filling her plate, she brought it to the table. Sunshine winked on the coffee pot and found raven lights in Paul's hair, and the weather being an eternally down-to-earth topic, Domini remarked that the storm had cleared the air and it looked like being a nice day.

"Shall we drive into Looe—there is a small jalopy of sorts in the garage we can use, or shall we walk along the headland?" Paul asked, little smile lines creasing the skin at the sides of his tawny eyes as they dwelt on her.

"Let's walk," she said at once.

"Good, I feel like a walk myself." He poured her coffee for her, and as he handed her the cup and saucer their fingers brushed, their eyes met, and Domini caught her breath. "The shadows have gone from your eyes this morning, Domini," he said, and for a moment it seemed to her that she saw them reflected in his eyes. But it could only have been her imagination, for the next moment he was smiling boyishly.

"I am glad to see you are none the worse for your ducking in the sea," he half laughed.

"No—I'm fine." She didn't look at him as she broke a roll and buttered it. She could feel the sudden heat in her cheeks. "Are you all right, Paul?" she asked.

"I am fine, my little wife." He threw out his arms and stretched like a powerful, graceful cat. Domini recognised the diamonds and anchors on his sweater as a Whinneyfield pattern and she asked him if he had ever been to Scotland.

"I have been to many places," he replied, and he leant his elbows on the table and watched her as she tucked into her breakfast. "But I am always glad to get home to Andelos. The sun is really hot there, Domini, and you will have to take care that you don't burn that English skin of yours."

Her pulse gave a nervous little leap at his mention of the island, where her future awaited her. "I shall lie about on the beach as much as possible and try to get as tawny as you," she said.

"You dare to spoil that lovely skin!" He rested his chin on his interlaced hands and his quirk of a smile made her notice how really well shaped his mouth was. "You belong to me now, Madame Stephanos, white skin and all."

"Of course," she mocked, "you snatched me like a Sabine, didn't you?"

"Domini," all at once an almost diffident note crept into his deep voice, "you don't regret last night, do you? You looked so lovely and beguiling—I could not leave you." He shrugged his wide shoulders. "I know I am not the easiest man in the world to know and to get along with, but I think I can make you reasonably happy—if you will let me."

She met his eyes and remembering again the shared and unexpected happiness of the wedding night that had evolved so strangely out of a tormented day, she let him find her hand with his. Let him touch his gold marriage ring and the frozen-blue sapphire below it. "Tell me some more about the island," she coaxed.

Never before had she asked him about his home and his people with such eagerness, and now she learned that he had had a younger brother who had died.

31

eighteen months ago; and a young stepsister, who lived with his Aunt Sophula and her son Nikos in a house above the harbour of Andelos. His aunt had been married to a sea-captain. Ships and the sea were in the blood of all the Stephanos's, and Nikos would be made a partner in Paul's shipping line when he reached the age of twenty-one.

"What is your sister's name, Paul?" Domini hadn't known he had a sister, and now as she studied him over the rim of her coffee cup she realised how little she knew about him, this complex being who could be so ruthless, yet whose kisses last night had made her forget everything but the moment. "How old is Kara?"

"Kara is sixteen," he smiled. "She is a young devil at times, but as lively and loveable as a wild fawn."

"I know so little about you and yours, Paul," Domini said, and her eyes dwelt on the scar that marred his right temple. "How did you get scarred, for instance?"

"Ah, that is a long story," he shrugged. "I will tell you one day, perhaps, but not this morning."

His mouth smiled, but his eyes remained serious, and obeying a sudden compulsion Domini rose and went round the table to him. He reached for her in silence and pulled her down into his arms and searched her face with his eyes before turning the search to a kissing one. Domini had not known how sensitive her skin was, and somewhat in the manner of a child enjoying the novelty of discovery she presented each part of her face for the touch of her husband's warm mouth.

This is Paul, she thought wonderingly, then his name broke from her as his mouth came down hard on hers. She dropped through layers of time with this stranger to the days when the Grecian gods took what they wanted and were fearfully punished for it. Did she, in the midst of his kisses, hear the Fates laughing? Perhaps, for suddenly her arms were locked tightly,

32

almost protectively about him, as though she felt instinctively that he was going to be punished in some
awful way.

There was a tap at the door, a discreet moment's wait,
then Yannis came into the room. Domini blushed and
attempted to pull out of her husband's arms, but he
held her on his lap without embarrassment as Yannis
asked if they intended to use the car that was available
in the garage. It was dusty and needed a hose down, he
added, but the task would not take him long.

Paul said they would not be needing the car; they
were going for a walk as far as Looe, and they would
have lunch there.

Yannis nodded, and couldn't quite keep his usual
gravity of expression as his eyes dwelt on Domini in his
master's arms, her cheeks like wild roses. "Another matter is the couch, sir. I have not been able to remove the
stains. The sea water, and the fabric so delicate—like a
woman's skin."

"Not to worry, Yannis." Paul smiled briefly, and rose
to his feet still holding Domini. "Perhaps Lita could find
a cover to throw over the couch for the time being. I
shall recompense the people from whom I rented the
villa, and as it happens we will not be here a week after
all. I have telephoned to change our plane reservations,
and we will be flying on to Athens tomorrow morning."

Yannis' look of surprise was echoed in Domini's eyes
as she glanced up into Paul's suddenly impassive face.
"Why the change of plans?" she asked breathlessly.

"Let us say that I am homesick for my house on the
eagle's crag." He touched the delicate indentation at the
base of her firm, shapely chin. "I cannot wait, little wife,
to show you the island of Andelos."

He could have been speaking the truth, of course,
but Domini was beginning to know that when Paul had
so impassive an expression he was either annoyed about

something, or worried. She felt disturbingly certain that he was worried about something right now—and that it was connected with her.

They set out for Looe half an hour later. It was a sparkling spring day, with an exhilarating breeze blowing along the headland above the grey Cornish sea. Always an outdoor person, Domini couldn't help but respond to the weather, the countryside, and the man who walked at her side.

She felt like a bride today, and she and her tall, bold husband were treated to quite a few admiring glances as they entered the small town of Looe and made their way towards the bank.

They were about to collect those cheques which her cousin had forged, and Domini thought with wonder of that terrified creature — herself — who had rummaged through Paul's belongings last night, feverishly telling herself that if she found and destroyed them, she would be free to run away from Paul. She glanced sideways at him. The sun was glistening on his hair, and he wore sunglasses. He had told her that his eyes were only really at rest in a muted light and that he suffered from rather bad headaches if he didn't keep his eyes covered while he was out in the sunshine. With his eyes shielded he seemed again the enigmatic stranger who had invaded her life and forced her into the bonds of matrimony with him. Mysterious bonds which there was no severing— until death should claim one of them!

While he went into the bank, Domini passed the time looking at a quaint collection of knick-knacks jumbled together in the small-paned window of a nearby antique shop. On impulse she went into the shop and asked the price of a small brass paperweight in the shape of a unicorn. She wanted to give it to Paul—for some odd, feminine reason.

Paul was coming across the road from the bank as she

came out of the shop, and she ran to meet him, her wild-honey hair blowing back from her eager face and the sleeves of her blouse fluttering below her cardigan, which she wore cape-like. "Look," she held out the unicorn, "do you like him?"

He smiled down at her. "Have you been treating yourself to a toy?" His deep, foreign voice was filled with laughing indulgence. "How much was it? I will pay for it."

"You won't, you know." She looked indignant. "He's for you. When I've cleaned him up, he'll look as smart as a new penny."

Paul took the unicorn and turned it about in his long fingers. "You really want *me* to have him, Domini?"

She nodded. "Call him a—wedding present. I-I couldn't afford anything dearer."

"He's dear enough," Paul murmured. He had replaced his sunglasses upon leaving the bank so she couldn't read his eyes, but she knew from the rough, hurried deepening of his voice that he liked her quaint little present.

"Here are the cheques, Domini." He showed her a long buff envelope, and a smile twisted his lips. "But I fear I cannot burn them in the middle of Looe High Street."

"We'll wait until we get back to the villa." Her heart suddenly felt as though it were beating in her throat. She wanted the cheques destroyed, out of her life for ever, but she felt she had to show Paul that she trusted him—at last.

"No, it must be finished!" There was a sudden steely note in his voice, and when he glanced round and noticed a nearby litter-bin, he strode to it and there he ripped the cheques into dozens of tiny pieces and scattered them like so much confetti over the orange peel, soggy ice-cream wrappers and apple covers.

One piece fluttered out of the bin and came to rest near Domini's left foot. When she glanced down at it, she saw clearly the deep slanting writing which Douglas had copied. She saw Paul's surname and her heart jolted as she realised that Stephanos was now her name as well.

They lunched at a quaint old eating-house in Looe, and afterwards they found a deserted cove below the headland and lazed on the sand. Domini lay curled in the hard crook of Paul's arm, listening to the sea and the deep, mysterious beat of her husband's heart against her cheek. The thought drifted across her mind that she might yet come to conflict with this man for snatching her away from Fairdane with all the presumption of a soldier of fortune, but right now she felt sun-warmed and relaxed in his company.

In a while he said to her, his fingers meshed in her soft hair: "Domini, I am going to ask you to make me a promise, and when you have made it, I shall expect you to abide by it."

She gazed up at his face. It had grown stern, and she was suddenly aware that he was still very much a stranger to her; that the breadth of his shoulders and the bold strength of his face still held the power to un-nerve her. "What sort of a promise must I make, Paul?" she asked, drowsy in the sun, pliant.

"To stay with me, no matter what happens between now and tomorrow when we leave England for Greece," he replied.

She sat up and pushed her honey hair back from her eyes. Out at sea a black cormorant dived upon its prey and flew to a rock with the struggling fish in its powerful beak. There on the rock it fed brazenly in the sun.

Domini drew her gaze back to Paul's dark face. "What could happen, Paul?" she asked, and the sun

36

seemed to grow cooler and she drew her cardigan around her shoulders.

"You could grow to hate me again." He watched her bite her lip and a cynical smile touched his arrogant mouth. "I see you think so as well?"

"Paul," she reached for his arm and gripped it, "you're frightening me. We've been happy today — it could go on."

"Who can tell about the future?" He shrugged and shadows seemed to touch the corners of his mouth as he picked up the brass unicorn and dusted sand from it with his fingers. "Do you know what the unicorn symbolises, Domini?"

She shook her head, and felt cold fingers of apprehension clench round her heart at his sudden change of mood. Not ten minutes ago he had been holding her in the sand and kissing the breath out of her, now he looked strangely melancholy. The look was intensified because he had replaced his dark glasses.

"A unicorn," he said, "symbolises the most elusive thing in the world — true happiness. He is a creature fashioned from the fabric of dreams, and happiness, too, is fashioned from the same fabric. For some it can be rent by pain and disaster, but never really destroyed. For others, if there is a flaw in the fabric from the very beginning, it can fall into irreparable fragments at the first touch of disaster. The fabric of our happiness has a flaw in it, and we both know it, Domini."

She shivered at his words, and saw the sun flickering like a flame in a draught.

"I must have your promise that you will stay with me, come what may." He placed his hand over her left one.

His words held underchords. *Peine forte et dure,* she thought. The weight of guilt was making him speak like this, and her heart melted as her eyes took in his black, close-curled hair, the scar about which he wouldn't talk, and the mouth that felt so warm though it could look so hard.

"For better or worse you're my husband," she said to him. "We can't break the marriage bond whatever else we destroy."

"Then I have your promise," he insisted.

"You have my promise, Paul."

He gave a little sigh, then slipped a cheroot between his lips and fired the tip. But still his thoughts were abstracted, for the flame of the match had burned down to his fingertips before he shook it out.

Domini watched him, glad when after a few minutes he began to look more relaxed. "You aren't entirely Greek, are you, Paul?" she said suddenly.

He had been sitting in profile, now he turned to look at her. "How can you tell?" he asked, sounding faintly amused.

"By your eyes—when I can see them. And your build."

"My grandmother was English." He broke into a smile that showed his firm white teeth. "What has my build to do with my not being a hundred per cent Greek? Were not the ancient Greeks tall men?"

"Apollo must have been very tall," she smiled, then glanced down and filtered sand through her fingers. "Is that why you chose to marry an Englishwoman, because of your grandmother?"

"Not entirely." His fingers found hers in the sand. "British women have a certain magic, a cool and tantalising quality."

"You mean we don't put everything in the shop window," she half laughed.

"Just so," he smiled. "Always a man can expect the unexpected from them."

"Have you known many of my countrywomen, Paul?"

"Do I detect a certain jealousy?" he mocked.

"No . . ." Then she gave a nervous laugh as his fingers gripped hers. She couldn't escape them and was drawn close against his chest. "You barbarian!" She hid her face against him, scorched by shyness of the feelings aroused in her as she felt and breathed the maleness of him.

"Ultra-civilised people are not very real, my Sabine." He spoke in her hair. "Do I still frighten you? Am I so sinister, scar and all, after last night? Come, you were not frightened when I held you so close and our hearts beat as one."

"I—can't talk about it," she said in a shy, muffled voice. "I have no Greek in me."

"Not even in your heart?" She felt his chest lift under her burning cheek, then the half smoked cheroot was flicked from his fingers and as both his arms came round her she went boneless. It was both an alarming and an exciting sensation, but this time when he kissed her, he seemed to be laying claim to her. And as her soft mouth suffered the aggresson of his, she felt she would never understand him, or the forces that drove him.

What was it he wanted? Her love? But how could she tell him she loved him, when she didn't know herself what she really felt for him?

They went home to the villa in the fading sunshine, and as they entered the hall their eyes fell simultaneously on a yellow envelope on the letter salver beside the telephone.

It was a telegram. It was for Domini, and she opened the envelope with fingers that were suddenly nerveless. Paul watched her as she read the telegram, his face an impassive mask when at last she glanced up at him. She looked him over from head to foot, and it was as though she had been asleep and dreaming for the past eighteen hours. Now she was awake again. Awake to the hate that had only slumbered in her for a while.

"It is from your uncle, of course?" Paul spoke almost casually.

She handed the telegram to him, without speaking. It read: "Know about cheques from Doug. Phoned Paul last night. Darling, come home!"

"So my uncle phoned here last night?" Domini said coldly.

"That is so, my dear." He folded the telegram with fingers that were utterly steady.

"And knowing Doug had told his father about what he had done, you deliberately came to me and—and—"

"Not deliberately, Domini—and I don't think we will stand shouting at one another in the hall." He forcibly took her wrist and made her go with him into the lounge. There he closed the door and stood with his back against it.

"I came to you last night," he said quietly, "because you cried out in your sleep and I was anxious about you. I kissed you, but if you had repulsed me, just once, I should have returned to my own room. You did not repulse me, so I made love to you. Call me all the names you want to. Say, even, that I took advantage of you, but that will not alter the fact that you forgot to hate me last night, and that you have been sweet to me today.

"Ah, yes," he shrugged in that foreign way of his. "It was a stolen sweetness, but I would not have stolen it if you had not let me."

"Really?" She laughed, quite humourlessly, and his dark power and grace held no more enchantment for her. "You meant all along to enjoy your new toy— your new possession. You said so in this very room last night. I was to abide by my marriage vows, willingly or the other way, therefore it must have given you a lot of satisfaction, Paul, to have got what you wanted without a struggle. No wonder," her breath caught in her throat, "no wonder you laughed to yourself when I asked if I could go to sleep in your arms."

"Domini, no—"

"Don't touch me!" She took a sharp step back from him as he moved. "Don't touch me again today or I shall be ill. Ill from my own sentimental stupidity. Ill from my own fantastic notion that you might, after all, be a man I could grow fond of. All day you must have been laughing at me! When you tore up those cheques, with the venom already extracted from them. When I let you kiss me in the sands of that cove. Well, if it's just the shape of me that you want, then you're welcome to what you bought. But all the money in the world won't buy my trust, or my love, and a wife without them is pretty cold comfort, Paul."

"Keep your love." His face was a taut sculpture, chiselled out of stone—as she felt certain his heart was. "Did I ever ask for it?"

"No, not in words," she threw at him. "But you're not quite so inhuman as to enjoy for very long the companionship of a wife who *hates* you. How could you dare, Paul, to take from me the freedom to choose Fairdane or Andelos?"

"It is in a Greek to dare the Fates themselves," he said cynically.

"The Fates!" she gasped, and thought wildly of her own strange conviction of that morning, when he had kissed her. But that was just superstitious nonsense! It would be his own conscience that would punish him for cheating her out of that telephone talk with her uncle.

"If I had let you speak to Martin Dane last night, you would have left me," Paul said, biting out the words. "Andelos would not have been your choice. You would have run home to Fairdane, and the old-fashioned charm and courtesy of your good uncle. Is that all you asked of life, to be a maid of all work in a house that is mortgaged to its gables?"

"Fairdane was my home," she said coldly. "I loved every brick of it. I can't promise to feel the same about your house on the eagle's crag."

"But all the same you will live there with me?"

"I made a promise." She thrust up her firm chin. "I don't go back on my promises."

"Thank you, Domini," he said.

"Don't thank me, Paul." Her eyes were a frozen blue as they dwelt upon his dark face. "You might live to regret that you ever came to Fairdane and met me."

Tiredly, then, she brushed past him, pulled open the door and crossed the hall to the stairs. As she mounted them she had to hold on to the banister rail, for suddenly her legs felt weak and shaky. She was glad when she reached her room, where she fell across the bed and pressed her face to the cold silk of the cover.

She couldn't weep. Tears had set like ice in her, and the sweetness of today had turned to bitterness. The rings on her slim hands felt heavy. Manacles, she told herself. Shackles that bound her to a man without a heart. A man who had forced her into a loveless disaster of a marriage.

He had talked himself about the flaw in the fabric of their relationship. He had said that the first touch of disaster would rend it and ruin it. He had known she would never forgive him for deceiving her, for making a mockery of her trusting surrender last night. A shudder ran through her as she rememebred the words she had whispered.

"Keep your arms around me, Paul. Let me fall asleep in them."

CHAPTER FOUR

NO matter how strong was Domini's desire to shut herself in her room and not have to see Paul, ever again, she found herself automatically dressing for dinner when the time came. Domini was very British. She couldn't crawl away into a dark corner and hide herself because she had been wounded. She had to put on a bold face to tackle her enemy with the remnants of pride and courage he had left her.

Paul, watching her unobtrusively across the dining-table, was aware that there had never been so wide a gulf between them. She was polite. She listened, and answered him, as he told her about the various cruising ships which his company owned. She even managed to smile a little at some of his amusing anecdotes about the passengers.

That stark and hurtful scene in the lounge might never have taken place — but for the dark pain he glimpsed in her blue eyes now and again.

After dinner they went to the lounge, where Paul had set up a film projector and a screen. He entertained her by showing a selection of travel films he had made himself, a hobby of his. They were full of lovely views, but there wasn't a shot that showed him with a party of friends, or even one female companion. When he finally switched off the projector and turned on a lamp, Domini said to him: "Do you always go around on your own when you're on holiday?"

He poured out sherry and smiled a little as he handed her one of the fluted glasses. "I like—as you English would put it—to mooch about on my own. It is a harmless eccentricity, no? Anyway, I always take Yannis along for company, and because I am too lazy to keep my own clothes in order."

She studied him under her lashes, coolly, impersonally, and she told herself that a man with his looks had not always spent his evenings alone even if he spent his days alone. There must have been other women in his life; women who had felt his magnetism and been challenged to try to tame him. But there was no taming such as he!

"Tell me about Greece," she said on impulse. While he talked she could forget her painful thoughts for a while.

"*Stin iyia sou.*" He raised his wine glass to her, and lay back in his chair with the lamp slanting its ruby-shaded shadows over the forceful moulding of his profile. "Greece is a land of contrasts. Of sunshine laced with shadow; of hospitality and vengeance. Some parts are barren, others are rich with the wild grape and the fig, the olive and pine tree. Ah, the pines! They fill the dusk with their resinous scent, and at dusk the sea is like a cup of wine."

He fell silent and his tawny eyes brooded on the fire. "Greece is a land to be loved or hated, like its people. The old legends are alive still in its ruins, and to see the city of Athens now makes it hard to believe that not many years ago it was torn by forces very horrible. Brother fought against brother, and later many of our children were herded like small cattle across the cold mountains into Albania and other hostile countries. You were but a baby, Domini, when all that occurred."

"You could not have been so very old yourself, Paul." She spoke gently because she knew he loved Greece.

"I was old enough—to see much," he said, and his smile was dry—dry and sad in the way of autumn leaves when they fall from the trees to die on the ground. "Domini, I am not speaking like this in order to gain your sympathy."

"Of course not," she said. "It isn't sympathy you want from me, is it, Paul?"

A smile contorted briefly the compression of his lips. "I wonder if you believe in affinities," he said. "It could have been inevitable that we meet—for better or worse. What do you think?"

"I think the hidden powers are not always kind," she replied.

And now conversation became desultory between them. The pauses spacing their short remarks were growing longer, and each movement in the room was beginning to create a growing restlessness in both of them. When the wood shifted in the fireplace, scattering its sparks, their eyes sought the movement in unison. When the curtains stirred in one of those queer draughts that seem to invade a room when the fire burns low, their eyes again found the movement.

Domini clenched her hands together in her lap. Soon they must rise from their chairs, leave the room and go upstairs. They could not remain here indefinitely. The room itself, grown tired of human habitation, was willing them to go.

Then all at once the clock began to chime. It was midnight, and Paul got abruptly to his feet and Domini saw the sudden harshness of his face as he exclaimed: "Go upstairs, for the love of God! I am not going to touch you. I know you are shrinking from the very sight of me."

She rose to her feet and set aside her sherry glass. Her face was without expression. "Goodnight, Paul." The words were almost inaudible.

"Kalé nichta!"

She walked out of the room, slim in her blue jersey dress, dragging her feet a little like a tired child. As

Paul watched her go, and the door closed on her, his fingers slowly clenched on the stem of his wine glass. There was a small, sharp click as the stem snapped and the dregs of the wine spilled over his hand.

It was very much later when Domini heard him enter the adjoining room. She lay tense and she thought: "I mustn't cry out tonight . . . if I sleep." But in the end, worn out by her own torn emotions, she slept deeply, exhaustedly, until she was awoken by Lita with her morning tea.

They were leaving here at eight-thirty, but Domini just had to speak to her uncle on the phone before they left. A talk with him yesterday had been impossible. She had felt too upset to be able to speak composedly to Uncle Martin, but this morning a certain measure of calm was hers and she felt certain she could sound convincing when she told her uncle that she was looking forward to seeing the island where her husband had been born, and where they were going to live.

Paul was in the lounge checking over the luggage with Yannis when she dialled the number that would connect her with her girlhood home. She wanted desperately to assure Uncle Martin that there was no need for him to worry any more that Douglas would be prosecuted for the foolhardy thing he had done. She prayed silently that she would convince her guardian that she was happy married to Paul Stephanos.

Her husband came out of the lounge as she waited for the operator to connect her with Fairdane, and she watched his tall, dark-clad figure go up the stairs and along the landing to the lilac suite. He was leaving her to speak in privacy, but she felt no sense of gratitude. He could be magnanimous because he had got his own way, and that was all there was to it . . . "Uncle Martin?" The warmth flowed back into her voice. "How are you, dear?"

Domini and her uncle talked for fifteen minutes. He was *not* to worry about Doug, she said firmly. Everything was all right now, and she was sure he would steer clear of the gaming tables after—well, tangling with Paul—yes, Paul could be intimidating—no, of course he didn't intimidate *her*. What an idea!

She gave a laugh, and went on to say quickly that she had seen some home movies depicting Greece and it certainly looked an interesting and ruggedly beautiful country.

"I shall miss you, Domini." There was a gruff, moved note in her uncle's voice. "Are you sure—you're happy with Paul?"

She stared blindly at the wall above the telephone table, and fought not to give way to her fear of the life that lay ahead of her with a man who did not love her.

"He can be kind," she assured her uncle. "And he's a strangely lonely man . . ."

Paul, at that moment, was coming down the stairs. She saw from his face that the time had come for her to say goodbye to her uncle. Now a huskiness in her voice would not sound alarming to him, for there was no keeping back the tears any longer.

"Goodbye . . . goodbye . . . I'll write as soon as we arrive in Athens." The words echoed in her mind as she went out to the taxi with Lita and Yannis. A minute later, after locking up the villa, Paul joined them, the door of the taxi slammed and they were on their way to the airport. They were flying from a West Coast airport to Paris. In Paris they would board a jet bound for Athens.

After the confusion of their arrival at Athens airport, they drove in a cab to the Hellenic Hotel, classic as any temple, with a terrace restaurant, a pavilion for dancing, and where from the windows of their suite the Acropolis could be seen by starlight, and dawnlight. At both these times, Paul added, something of its legendary beauty could be seen again.

Yannis and his wife had been released from their duties so they could take a holiday; they were to go across to the island of Andelos in three weeks' time, a week before Paul and his bride were due to arrive there.

Domini felt nervous about being alone with Paul—a stranger's bride in a strange land—but it could not be avoided and she had to get used to him sooner or later.

She was tired after their long journey, so they ate in the sitting-room of their suite that evening and when Paul wished her *kalé nichta*, he bent his dark head and brushed a kiss across her cheek. Half a medal for being a good sport, she told herself, but much as she tried she couldn't keep her body from tautening at his touch. At once he turned away from her, looking impassive.

The Greek sun fairly leapt through her bedroom windows the following morning, waking her up with its brash golden stare.

They breakfasted on fruit juice, creamy butter and honey, and crisp rolls with sesame seeds scattered on their tops. Afterwards they ate amber-coloured figs with juicy purple centres, and drank Greek coffee. "Delicious," Domini murmured, and her eyes dwelt with pleasure on the lemon-flowers meshed in shiny leaves that cloaked their balcony.

"Don't drink your coffee to the dregs," Paul warned.

She nodded and toyed with the little cup. The dregs would be bitter, she knew, like so many things that seemed sweet at the time and yet left an aftermath that was embittering.

"What shall we do this morning?" he asked, leaning back in his cane chair to light a cigarette. Domini had shaken her head at his proffered case, but she couldn't avoid looking at him. His hair had a raven crispness under the sun; he wore a short-sleeved sports shirt and narrow slacks; and cigarette smoke wafted past his smoky-gold eyes so that they narrowed and had a tiger gleam.

"Some sightseeing would be nice," she said.

"Then I shall take you to the Plaka, the old part of Athens." His teeth showed white in a quick smile. "Wear sandals, for the paving stones are old and uneven. After a look round the shops, perhaps you would like to see the Acropolis?"

"Very much," she assured him, and saw a small Greek medal glitter in the opening of his shirt as he leant forward to tip ash off his cigarette. The medal against his chest stabbed her to a memory she was trying hard to forget . . . the feel of it against her in the darkness in the warmth of his arms . . .

She rose quickly to her feet. "I must go and comb my hair and put on some lipstick," she said, and she turned away from the table and went into her room, where the Venetian blinds cast tiger stripes as she ran a comb through her glossy hair and avoided her own eyes in the toilet-table mirror. Her hand shook as she applied lipstick and she had to wipe away a smear with a tissue and fill in anew with rose colour the shapely curves of her mouth.

Domini stared at her own mouth, with its sensitive upper lip and generous lower one. She felt it crushed, silenced and possessed beneath his mouth that had said, coldly: "Keep your love. Have I ever asked for it?"

Her face coolly composed, she stepped into a pair of walking sandals and latched them, then she took up her handbag, her sun-specs and a headsquare, and flicked a final glance over her reflection. She was slender and outwardly poised to her fingertips in tapering blue slacks and a cream overblouse. She wore no ornamentation but her rings, the plain gold band and the sapphire that was as blue as her eyes.

Domini Stephanos, she thought, and gave a little shiver at the strangeness of the name. The Domini Dane of only a few days ago was gone for ever, leaving only the shape and the face that had moved a man to ruthless lengths in order to gain possession of them. She swung away from the mirror, fingers curled round the strap of her shoulder-bag as she joined her husband for their sightseeing tour of the Plaka and the Acropolis.

The streets of the Plaka were shelving and narrow, filled with open-fronted, bazaar-like shops, Byzantine faces, and houses with jutting wooden balconies and small secretive patios.

She felt the guiding warmth of Paul's fingers at her elbow as he pointed out the garlic and peppers festooning a grocer's doorway, the strings of plimsolls, outside a shoeshop, the panniers and baskets of weird and wonderful fruits. There was a sponge-seller carrying a motley of sponges like vari-coloured balloons, and a melon boy trundling a cart loaded with the blue-green *kaboussia*. Paul bought slices of watermelon and after Domini had eaten her portion all her lipstick was gone with the juice and she looked like a teenager on holiday as she gazed round at the many people crowding this muddle of pungent, noisy, colourful streets.

"It's like Petticoat Lane," she laughed over her shoulder at Paul. "That sponge-seller will float away if the wind catches him."

"You are having fun?" He smiled and drew a little closer to her.

She nodded, for the Plaka held a gay and earthy magic that there was no withstanding, and now Paul caught at her melon-sticky fingers and held them as they mounted the uneven steps and passed *tavernas* where dignified old men sat over their wine and their

Turkish coffee and bit out the Greek words that made them sound as though they were arguing.

Greek matriarchs passed by with their slim daughters, and many of the young men were handsome and sporting black moustaches. Quite a few of them wore green-khaki uniforms; military service was compulsory, Paul told her, and when she glanced up at him she saw a shadow move across his face. It seemed to leave his scar etched sharp for a moment, then he glanced sideways into a shop and she couldn't see his eyes. His sunglasses were folded in the breast pocket of his shirt, for they were not necessary here where the fierce sun was shut out by the crowding roofs of houses and shops.

He paused outside the dim little shop, where there was a pile of embroidered slippers, handwoven straw handbags, and long strings of Greek 'worry' beads above trays of brooches and earrings. "Let me buy you a memento of our visit to the Plaka," Paul said, and he bent over the trinket trays. A man wearing a turban came out from the interior of the shop and stood watching as Paul selected a pair of lapis lazuli eardrops, heart-shaped and irresistibly pretty. He asked the Turk how much they were and after paying for them, he drew Domini into a nearby doorway and, looking earnest, he attached the tiny blue hearts to the lobes of her ears.

She gave her head a shake so she could feel them. "They're cute, Paul. They make me feel like your harem slave," she added.

But Paul didn't smile in return, he suddenly gripped her around the waist and tipped back her chin with his free hand. His mouth looked as hard as his arm felt, and his eyes blazed down into hers, tiger-gold. "Is that how you feel," he spoke in a low, savage voice, "like a harem slave whose favours are being bought with trinkets?"

She gazed up at him helplessly. "I never meant anything—I was joking," she faltered.

"The subconscious often speaks for us in words we *think* we don't mean," he said curtly. Then he let her go and in silence they continued their walk to the Acropolis. Domini felt tearful. His harem slave! The words had slipped out, destroying his moment of pleasure in giving her a small gift.

Still feeling rather small in her heart, Domini stood between the towering columns of the gateway of the Greek gods, looking up and up, taking in the rugged grace and grandeur of the columns that were like fingers pointing towards heaven.

Here on these giant steps a splendid scene was laid out, taking her breath, while a vagrant breeze teased her blouse and the wings of her hair.

"Come," Paul said, and he showed her the Portico of Maidens, where tourists aimed their cameras and touched the carving of tunics that seemed almost to move against the stone limbs of the Grecian maidens. Paul then showed her the ancient olive tree that still grew here—symbol of hope, he said, and her gaze was drawn to him as he stood on the great steps. The sun meshed him in gold, and there on his face was that look again, as though a savage memory was gripping him as he gazed down over the ancient capital of Greece.

He had his small Leica with him, and he took pictures of her seated on the ledge of the Parthenon, leaning against a truncated column, turning in profile to follow the winged quiver of a cicada. "Kara will expect us to bring home plenty of honeymoon pictures," he said, a caustic edge to his smile.

"Then we should have some taken together — to please Kara," Domini felt moved to say.

And with the friendly co-operation of an American tourist they stood side by side under a massive portico and he prepared to take several shots of them. "Say, fella," the American lowered the Leica, and broke into a coaxing grin, "I know you Greeks aren't demonstrative in public, but an arm about the little lady would look kinda nice."

Paul cast a sardonic look over Domini's face, then his arm encircled her slim waist and he drew her against the hard, male warmth of him. Her smile towards the camera was taut as her body within the circle of Paul's arm. She felt his fingers bite into her waist for a painful second, then the pictures were taken and he was walking away towards the American. "Mighty nice camera," said the tourist. "You can't beat a Leica for detail. Your wife should come out fine —just like one of those Grecian maidens in that frieze."

"*Efharisto.*" Paul gave the man his grave smile as he took his camera. "It was good of you to take the photographs."

"*Parakalo.*" The American looked pleased with himself for being able to say 'you're welcome' in Greek, then he grinned goodbye at them and sauntered away.

Paul shot a look at his wristwatch. "You must be hungry," he said. "Shall we eat at a *taverna*, or would you prefer to go back to the hotel?"

Not the hotel, not yet! A *taverna* would be noisy, lively, full of colourful strangers among whom she could lose herself for at least another hour. "I'd like to eat at a *taverna* and have a real Greek lunch," she said quickly.

"Come, then."

And as they went down the grass-grown steps, past a clump of wild blue flowers, she was aware of people looking at them. At the tall, handsome Greek and his British bride. So had it been in Cornwall, the day they had gone into Looe to collect those cheques. But that day Domini had felt the bubbles of a wild, sweet wine in her veins; now the bubbles were still and the wine had turned bitter.

CHAPTER FIVE

THEY were making for a *psistaria,* where grilled meats were served apart from fish, when someone called Paul's name and they found themselves surrounded by several animated people. They turned out to be a couple of business associates of Paul's accompanied by their wives, alarmingly well-groomed women wearing flowered hats, silk suits, and carrying very expensive handbags in gloved hands. They flicked dark eyes over Domini's casual attire and seemed rather shocked that the wife of an important businessman should go around dressed like a tourist.

Their husbands, on the other hand, smiled at her with frank delight and insisted that she and Paul join their party for lunch.

"You plan to lunch here, Kostes?" Paul gestured at the eating-house directly behind his friend, and he spoke in English because Domini did not understand much Greek as yet. Kostes, in accented English, replied at once that the place was celebrated for its Greek cooking and they were lunching there . . . yes, he nodded masterfully at his wife, despite her wish to go somewhere smarter where the food would be dressed up but tasteless.

"It took Kostes a long time to become a man of means," Angelica confided to Domini as they followed the men into the eating-house. "For years I wear patiently the shabby and unfashionable clothes, now when I have smart clothes to show off, he brings me to eat in a rough *taverna.* A Greek must be the master, you understand!"

Domini smiled and understood one thing only too well. In front of his friends Paul would expect her to put on a 'radiant bride' act, and it was hard to have to admit to herself that she didn't dare oppose his wishes.

He had his pride. What was *hers* in comparison?

Her eyes followed him, head and shoulders above the other two men, as a waiter led them to a table for six.

The *taverna* was a place that would have charmed Domini at any other time, in company less curious and unnerving. The chairs at the rustic tables were cane-seated, the rough walls were whitewashed and hung with strange gourds, instruments of folklore music, and a large flag-draped portrait of the handsome Greek king and his lovely young wife.

All around there was the bite of Greek conversation, overhung by a haze from the spits where chunks of lamb, veal and poultry were roasting over the pungent, glowing coals. Pots simmered on a large stove, and Domini was taken by Paul to choose her own soup, vegetables and meat. The other two women were having grilled *larks,* and she was secretly horrified. She could not have eaten those tiny birds if Paul had ordered her to. He didn't of course, and she saw a smile twitch on his lips as she said firmly that she would have grilled chops. She also fancied chips, and Paul at once ordered that they be freshly cooked. He gestured significantly at the dish of half-cold chips under a glass dome.

"The English do not like a warmed-up dish, no?" he said, and she was thinking that one over as they returned to their table, where Kostes was ordering *retsina,* the pine-flavoured white wine of Greece.

"You will not like it." Paul shook his head at Domini and ordered a St. Helena for her to drink with their *lakerda,* tender slivers of smoked fish they had decided on instead of soup.

Angelica and Myrrha were tucking into fish-roe paté, spreading it thickly on breadsticks and throwing questions at Domini as they ate with appetite. *"Chairete!"*

Kostes smiled across the table at her and raised his wine glass.

It was a word Domini understood, meaning 'be happy.' She smiled back at the amiable Greek and hoped it didn't show in her eyes that happiness had become just a word to her; a memory of freedom to enjoy life in peace at her beloved Fairdane, in the keeping of her gentle guardian.

Then her heart gave a wild beat as Angelica asked her—loud enough for all at the table to hear — how many children she hoped to have. Domini stared at a dish of brown olives with violet lights in them. Children —with Paul—

She caught a tawny sideways glance from him as she summoned a smile for Angelica and murmured a non-committal answer. The two Greek women exchanged knowing smiles. They thought her shy because she was British, and they kind-heartedly went on to talk about the plays to be seen at Epidaurus in the play season. "You must coax Paul to take you," Myrrha waved a lark's wing in her enthusiasm. "The seats of the amphitheatre are of stone, I warn you, but I always take along an air cushion which Spiros inflates for me. Last season we saw *Elektra*. What an experience that was, *kyria.*"

This was better. Domini was able now to relax over her grilled chops, crisp, piping hot chips and tight little green sprouts as she listened to Myrrha's vivid descriptions of the play.

For dessert, Domini chose pistachio ice-cream and as she spooned the delicious mouthfuls she was noticing the smile edging Paul's lips as he sat back expansively to enjoy a thin cigar and his *kaffés tourkikos*. She had evidently played her part to his satisfaction; her small confusions had been taken as evidence of bridal shyness, and no doubt it also pleased him that she had remained indifferent to the admiring glances her fair hair and complexion had attracted from men at nearby tables.

When she and Paul departed for their hotel, they took with them an invitation to Myrrha's house on Friday, and Angelica's on Sunday evening.

"They liked you," Paul said as the self-service lift at the Hellenic swooped them to their floor. "Kostes said in an aside that never had he seen eyes as blue as the Greek sea."

Domini lifted those deep blue eyes to her husband's dark face, and politely replied that she had liked his friends.

"Don't be on the defensive with me!" With a sudden frown he took her by the shoulders, his hands warm and hard through the thin material of her blouse. "Call me a Greek pirate, slap my face, but don't be always so— *polite*."

"I'll learn," she said stiffly. "Give me time, Paul."

"Time has a way of running away," he rejoined, and his profile had a set look as they walked to the door of their suite and he pushed the key into the lock with a hard thrust. Her heart gave a jolt. She knew in that moment that he would not remain aloof with her for much longer; he had the needs of a strong, emotional man, and she had already learned that he could be ruthless.

The following day their suite looked like a flower shop. The word had got around that Paul Stephanos was in Athens and that he had brought a British bride with him. Baskets of flowers kept arriving at the door, boxes of fruit and candy, *and* wedding gifts for young Madame Stephanos. Domini was but human and she couldn't help loving the flowers, and nibbling at the Turkish delight, the pistachio nuts and golden Corinth grapes.

Domini was intrigued by the gifts of liqueur glasses,

silver jam spoons and decorative little dishes, and Paul explained the Greek custom of guests being greeted by their hostess with a sweet preserve or a cordial. "Honey in the mouth," Domini smiled.

"Quite so." Paul's eyes dwelt on her mouth, and she turned at once to bury her nose in the dewy petals and furry, heart-shaped leaves of a mass of violets. "I love violets," she said.

There was silence from Paul, who had gone to the balcony doors to light a cheroot. She shot a glance over the violets at his broad shoulders and his dark pagan head, and she sensed from something rather tense about him that the violets had come from him.

She felt she ought to thank him, but the words wouldn't come. How had he known that these were her favourite flower? She had never talked to him about such things, and he had never seen her in the woods at Fairdane, curled in the fork of a beech tree above a bank of wild violets that burst into colour in the spring. That Domini would not have interested him—would she?

In the next few weeks she and Paul received lots of invitations to go out dining, dancing and driving. It was a gay whirl which she rather welcomed, for it saved her from thinking too much about the island of Andelos, where she would be alone with Paul in his house on the eagle's crag. The time to depart drew nearer each day, and there they would not arrive home late from a party or a drive. There Paul would not wish her a polite *kalé nichta* and turn from her to the loneliness of his own room.

The evening before they set out for Andelos, they attended a dance on a yacht in the harbour of Athens. The big craft was to be festooned with fairy lights, and

59

dancing was on the main deck under the stars, with a small orchestra providing the music.

Domini wore that evening a Grecian-draped dress of sea-lavender chiffon over silk. Her hair was swirled up in a Grecian style, with tiny violets secured in the honey-soft chignon. Before she and Paul departed for the dance, he latched about her arm a silver bracelet with an amethyst clasp. She fingered it. It was like a slave bracelet and she knew he was having a tilt at her for what she had said in the market-place of Plaka when he had pinned the little blue hearts to her ear-lobes.

"Here in Greece you have grown even lovelier," he said. "Our pagan sunshine has warmed your skin to honey—tell me, do I not get a kiss for my gift?"

She lifted her face like an obedient little girl, and he laughed softly against her cheek as he warmed it with his lips. "You fear the Greek when bringing gifts, don't you?" he said mockingly. "What have I to hide?"

She looked into his tawny eyes—the eyes were said to be the windows of the heart, but all Domini saw in Paul's was an enigmatic smile and her own minuscule reflections in the brilliant pupils. He had arresting eyes. Like the rest of him they were handsome and untamed. She could, had he not been the husband she feared, have admired him in his crisp white dinner-jacket over a white silk shirt, dark cummerbund and tapering trousers.

Apollo carved in teak, she thought, as he adjusted her peplos-like cloak and they stepped out of their suite like any normally happy couple setting out for an evening's fun.

Domini liked to dance. She had learned how to at boarding-school, which had been a progressive one, and Barry had taken her dancing several times. Barry came into her mind as on the fairy-lit deck of the *Silver Witch*

60

she felt the guiding pressure of Paul's hand in the small of her back as they danced without words. There had been words and whispers with Barry all the time, under the prisms of the big witchball whirling in the ceiling of the seaside club where they used to meet. She had to creep out of school after dark with the help of a dormitory friend, so that her meetings with Barry had a romantic secretiveness about them from the very start.

Strange, that here in Greece she should be thinking about him so much. She supposed she had a secret longing to be with him instead of Paul.

Domini closed her eyes and tried to pretend that she was in Barry's arms—but these arms were harder, and had she laid her head against the crisp tuxedo her cheek would have been near Paul's heart instead of resting in the comfortable hollow of his shoulder.

"You dance well," he murmured above her head. "I had no idea you entertained to any great extent at Fairdane."

"We didn't," she replied. "There just wasn't money enough. I learned how to dance at boarding-school."

"You seem accustomed to being led by a man rather than another girl," curiosity tinged his voice. "I have noticed this before. You almost give yourself in dancing, Domini."

Her heart gave one of those jolts that only he could cause, as though an electric current ran from his frame into hers. It was oddly disquieting. "You're forgetting—my cousin," she said. "When Doug was at home, we often danced to the old gramophone in the hall. The oak floors at Fairdane are like silk with age."

"Ah, Douglas!" Still that curious note was in his voice. "Yes, I suppose you must have cared a lot for that young—man."

The music ceased, someone put into her hand a glass of sparkling Greek wine, and during the next couple of hours Domini danced with other men while Paul went off somewhere. "Several of the Greeks are playing cards down in the stateroom," a young American told her. "Greeks like to gamble, so I've been told."

"Only they?" she murmured, her thoughts flying to her cousin. Did Paul really think she had married *him* because she cared for Doug beyond the bonds of kinship? How odd—and how frighteningly acute of him to guess that she had often danced with a man she cared for!

Cared for? Did that mean that love for Barry had never really flickered out in her heart? What a hopeless love when she had no idea where he was, but knew that if they should meet again it would have to be as strangers because she was no longer Domini Dane.

Some time later Domini grew weary of dancing and she found a narrow flight of steps and mounted them to a secluded corner of another deck of the yacht. Here she stood alone at the rail, a breeze fingering her hair and her cheek, coins of moonlight dappling the sea, the spars and rigging of other boats and caiques etched darkly against the sea sparkle. There was in the seductive murmuring of the water a gentle melancholy that found an echo in Domini. The sounds of music and laughter drifted up from the deck where people danced, and with her eyes lifted to the stars she wondered about her future with Paul.

She gave a cold shiver as in a silver flurry a star suddenly fell out of the sky, while in that moment a deep voice said: "You look as cool and distant as those stars, Domini."

In his silent-footed way Paul had come up behind her. She didn't turn round and his breath stirred her hair as his hands curved warm and strong over her shoulders. She stood very still, only her heart had movement, and the nerve that twitched in her lower lip.

"You enjoy a little solitude now and again, don't you?" he murmured.

She nodded.

"You will like the island, Domini." His voice, even his hands on her shoulders were quiet, but she felt it was a waiting quiet. "It is a place made for those who like the wild, the free, the unspoiled. Listen to the sea. It holds a siren's song."

"Can you hear the sea from your house?" she asked.

"From our house, Domini." He let her go and leaned against the deck rail with his back to the sea. His eyes, when she glanced at him, were leaping and lambent as a nocturnal cat's; his black hair was ruffled, he had been drinking wine and playing cards, and her throat tightened nervously at something she glimpsed in him— a smouldering air of recklessness.

"You are fingering your pearls like worry beads," he mocked. "Why, little Greca, are you so afraid of me?"

"Isn't it natural to fear what one doesn't understand?" She had brought down her hand from her pearls and her fingers curled over the shiny deck rail.

"It is true we Greeks are never easy of understanding." His teeth showed in a narrow smile. "Much of what we feel is submerged—but all the same it is there, the fire of the volcano, or the ice below the sea. But surely the same can be said about the British? You as you stand there — do you think I don't find you a mystery? Domini, the girl with the rare and lovely name to match her person. Domini, who will only reap her vengeance when I prove to her I am a devil by taking what she will not give me."

He put back his pagan head and laughed in the face of the moon. "Well, 'oracle of brides,' here is one to make you wonder at . . ."

"You're drunk!" Domini exclaimed, her face taut with dislike. She was about to walk away from him when, lithe and quick as a tiger, he pinioned both her wrists with one steely hand and tipped back her face with the other. "My little tempest," his eyes were alight with raw-gold flame, "yes, this I will have——" and his mouth crushed hers, bittersweet from the wine of Greece, violent and drugging, taking, forcing, leaving her with seared lips as she fled away from him, down the steps and back among the civilised.

In the cab that took them to the hotel, they sat coldly apart. Domini did not look at him in the lift, standing icily withdrawn in her Grecian gown and cloak, her eyes as frozen as the sapphire on her left hand. They bade each other goodnight in the sitting-room, then Domini walked into her room and closed the door with a curt little click. There was a key in the lock, and even as her fingers were moving towards it, she withdrew them. To lock her door would be an open admission of the deep fear in her heart. She wouldn't give Paul *that* satisfaction.

Mental unrest has a way of disturbing one's sleep with unnerving dreams. Domini could not have said afterwards what her dream was about, but she awoke suddenly from it to find her face wet with tears. She sat up in bed, tasting the salt of her tears on her mouth, and she saw at once beyond her bedroom windows a queer, reddish flickering in the sky. As her heart quickened with alarm, she threw back her bed-covers and ran to see what was causing that orange glare.

She pulled open the balcony doors and in her filmy nightdress she stood outside, staring down to where the torch of a fire lit up the harbour. A caique or a yacht was ablaze, and she heard firebells and saw sparks rise above the flames into the sky. She didn't hear her door open, but all at once Paul had joined her on the balcony.

"Could it be the *Silver Witch?*" she gasped.

"Something large is aflame down there," he crisped.

"What a shame if it is the *Witch!* Such a lovely boat —and I do hope your friends got off safely."

He went to the balcony parapet and peered down hard at the harbour, as if calculating the exact position in which his friends' yacht must lie. "No, it is not the *Witch*. She is moored farther along in the basin," he said at last. "What a blaze! It may be a cargo boat of some sort."

He turned and the reflections of the flames bathed him in their leaping light, and as he came towards Domini he seemed in his dark silk pyjamas to tower over her in a devil-like way. He muttered something in Greek as she involuntarily stepped back into her room, and she gave a little wince as he followed and closed the balcony doors none too quietly. "I—I'm glad that awful fire is not on the *Witch*," she said, and hated the slight shake in her voice.

He didn't answer and she forced herself to glance up at him. He stood framed by the fire glow, and he was assessing her pale slender shape in the blue filminess of her nightdress. It was a look that made Domini feel naked.

"You once accused me of buying you, Domini," he said. "You really believe it, don't you?"

She swallowed dryly, feeling the frantic clamour of her frightened heart even as some devil prodded her to say recklessly: "What is it, Paul, do you think it time you collected interest on those torn-up cheques?"

She heard him catch his breath, then he moved a step nearer and the room seemed darkly filled with his tall, wide-shouldered figure. He gave a low, savage laugh. "Yes, my dear, the time has come, I think, for you to stop playing the shrinking violet. I have had enough of *that,* especially when I know that there is another side to your cool beauty and your pride—"

"You want to humble my pride, is that it, Paul?" she threw at him, finding the pluck to defy him even as terror seemed to have locked a grip on her legs. She couldn't move, was utterly incapable of it as with one of his sudden lithe movements he reached for her and swung her up into his arms. Blindly, wildly, she began to struggle for freedom. "Paul, let me go!" Her fingers raked upwards into his scar and his tousled hair. "I—I shall hate you—"

"Don't you hate me already, my little tempest?" And there was in his eyes—as the flames outside flared up anew and lit the sky—a look of utter possessiveness. Like Apollyon, the destroying angel, he carried her into his own room and kicked the door shut behind them. His wide shoulders seemed like wings spread above her as he laid her down on the bed, shutting out the world as his arms enclosed her.

"I want you, Domini, whether you hate me or not." His mouth was in her hair as he whispered the fierce words. "I want a wife, not a polite and lovely stranger."

"We'll never be anything but strangers," she said with equal fierceness.

"A Sabine with her Roman, eh?" He laughed against her throat, then took her mouth . . .

Domini stirred awake just before dawn. A faint cool light was seeping into the room and she cautiously turned her head, her hair a wild-honey tangle, and gazed at Paul in sleeping defencelessness beside her. His black lashes shadowed his cheeks, scrolls of crisp hair were adrift on his forehead, and never before had she seen his mouth relaxed like that—almost gentle, she could have thought, if she hadn't known that gentleness was something alien to his nature.

One arm was still about her, but it had relaxed and

very carefully she slipped free of it, her heart coming into her mouth as he muttered something in his sleep and stirred a little, then as she frozenly watched him he settled down again, and Domini crept away as though from a sleeping tiger.

In her own room, Domini slipped into a robe and sat down by a window. She watched as the pink fingers of dawn began to paint the Acropolis . . . it was an utterly beautiful scene that she watched with a hook in her heart.

CHAPTER SIX

DOMINI never forgot her first glimpse of Andelos, which they came to in Paul's cabin-cruiser with a young sailor from the island at the helm, and a cheeky *mikro* acting as galley-boy.

The island rose suddenly out of the blue Ionian Sea, etched so clearly by the clarity of Greek light that its lyre-shape was plain to the eye. Domini's hands curled over the rail where she stood — Andelos, occupied long ago by the Venetians and Romans, where signs of their occupation must still linger, setting its stamp on the people as she knew it was set on the man who was taking her to his own fastness on a crag above the narrowing end of the island. The wild and lonely part.

'Draw near with heart unsullied to the house of Apollo, O Stranger,' came into her mind. 'And hence when the god is in the land the lyre, too, brightens into a summer strain concerning him.'

She thought it very possible, for those two young Greeks couldn't leap fast and eagerly enough to carry out his orders, and no doubt all the other islanders respected, even loved the man who had provided them with a well-run hospital, a school for their children where there were showers and a gym, *and* a library. Paul had not told her of these things. Angelica and Myrrha had been her eager informants.

Beside her Paul was leaning on the rail in a nonchalant attitude. His white shirt was deeply open at the throat, sunglasses concealed his eyes, and the sea air had roughened his black hair into tiny crisp curls at his nape and temples. They weren't touching, yet Domini could feel him with her nerves. Her body and her heart were still sensitive to his ruthlessness of three nights ago, and during these days at sea it had taken all her courage to behave naturally with him.

"We grow near to the island," he said. "Are you looking forward to seeing your new home?"

He knew well enough what was really in her heart . . . a longing for freedom such as those sea birds had as they dived with the wind. "I imagine your house on the eagle's crag to be an interesting one," she replied. "Has it been in your family for many years?"

"My grandfather had it built." Paul lifted his cheroot and the tangy smoke drifted to Domini's nostrils. "It was he and his brother Loukas who started the Stephanos Shipping Line. During the rebellion the business suffered serious setbacks, as did everything and everyone in Greece, but in time we tacked out of the troughs and sailed into smoother waters."

He fell quiet for a minute or so, and out of the corner of her eye Domini saw him staring almost sternly at the approaching island. Then he went on abruptly: "The house to which I am taking you has no deep roots in the past, as Fairdane has. It is, you might say, the concrete expression of man's victory in soaring above the arid soil . . . Greek soil is often arid, and life is very hard for many of my countrymen."

"But the clan Stephanos made it," she said flippantly.

She felt his glance and knew there was steel in it.

"We made it by sheer hard work, and never did one of us stoop to stealing."

"Not one, Paul?" There was a quiet note of meaning in her voice, and it gave her an inward sense of triumph to be able to barb her darts as well as he.

She watched the endlessly running crests of the ocean, lapping and overlapping, like liquid pewter under the gold of the sun . . . like thrills of pain and pleasure they mounted, fell and were born anew.

"The sea embodies everything," her husband murmured beside her. "Like the womb of life itself, holding tumult, energy and peace."

"The sea is cruel," she rejoined. "It takes as much as it gives."

"There is cruelty in everything, even in joy, and we have to accept this." He flicked his cheroot stub into the water, and then Domini felt his hand on her arm, sliding the bare length of it to her wrist, which he shackled with his hard fingers. "I know you find it hard, my romantic Sabine, to accept the fact that those hours in my arms were not entirely hateful the other night."

"Don't let's talk about *that!*" She tried to pull free of his grip, but he held her a prisoner with arrogant ease.

"Come, I insist on an answer." He gave her wrist a shake.

"They were what you wanted — those hours." She tossed back her head and there were blue flames in her eyes. "Yes, I can give you *that,* Paul, for what it's worth. My heart is my own."

"You think of our marriage in terms of tyranny, eh?" His eyes held hers. "Well, let me tell you, Domini, that if you lived with a man you loved you would find that there is a time for fighting, a time for being close, and a time for being distant. Hate and love are not such strangers to each other, and the obscure gallantries and repressions of romance are for reading about in books."

"To expect romantic gallantry from you, Paul, would be adolescent," she rejoined. "I am receiving all that I expected when I vowed to obey you."

"And remember that honour was among those vows," he said with a hint of menace.

"It is a pity you didn't remember, Paul." Her hair blew in the sea wind like a wild-silk pennant; her eyes were filled with the blue of the Greek sky and ocean . . . a nerve flickered into life beside Paul's mouth as he

70

gazed down at her. His eyes moved over her Cretan embroidered blouse worn over sailcloth trews, the wind flattened the silk to her, caressed her, frolicked with her hair, brought a flush of carnation to her cheeks.

"The people of Andelos will think me the luckiest man on earth," he said ironically.

"I wish I were plain!" she threw into the wind.

"Do you, my little tempest?" He put back his black head and laughed deeply. "Plain—beautiful—you would still be Domini."

She heard him, but her gaze was caught by the glimmering movement of a large sea creature moving quite close to the boat. "Are there sharks in Greek waters?" she asked, pointing towards that flash of a flipper in the water.

"It is a dolphin." He leaned over to watch the gliding, circling, then lovely leaping shape, his arm slung about Domini's waist. She was delighted with the dolphin, the first one she had ever seen, and she turned to smile brightly at Paul. "Apollo's desire of the sea," she quipped.

"Apollo had many desires, and many battles to win," he said dryly. "Dolphins come to sport in the lagoon of our private beach, so you are assured of some entertainment during your stay at the house on the eagle's crag."

"Won't we always be there?" She laughed at the leaping antics of the dolphin in the water.

"Not always," Paul said quietly.

"Business, I suppose, makes it necessary for you to travel?"

"Yes," he agreed. "I shall be making a certain journey in a few months' time."

Her attention was mainly on the dolphin when he spoke, but something about his tone of voice made her glance at him. There was no reading his eyes behind those sunglasses, but she wondered if he had been hinting that she was but a caprice and in time he would let her go . . .

The hook in her heart seemed to pierce deeper . . . his to hold while it pleased him, as he was holding her right now, a hard tanned arm possessively about her, his hand pressing against her waist.

Their boat by-passed the harbour of Andelos, for they were heading for the lagoon that was part of Paul's property, but Domini saw enough of the harbour to be able to take in its Venetian-like aspect. Colourful fishing caiques were tied up there, houses mounted in tiers from the pebbled shore, their white walls soaked in Greek sunshine. There came across the water as they passed the singing of a young fisherman; strangely, hauntingly his song followed them until it was lost.

"What does he sing about?" Domini asked, intrigued.

"About the girl he hopes to marry when his sisters are settled," Paul told her, a hint of amusement in his voice. "Not quite as romantic as you expected, eh? But that is how it often is in Greece; if the son of a poor family is the main breadwinner, then he must provide until his sisters are married off."

"How hard for the poor boy," Domini murmured. "No wonder he sounded so sad."

"Ah, but his girl loves him," Paul said dryly, "He knows she will wait for him, and that her heart will store up love as sealed wine stores up sweetness."

Domini gave a little shiver at the primitive beauty of the words . . . but did a waiting love always grow sweeter? Surely such an idea held the essence of romance, yet Paul had said he had no belief in romance.

The lagoon was guarded by a reef of dark rocks, and the day being calm the blue waters merely creamed their bows as they entered through a narrow channel that in rough weather, Domini thought, would be hazardous to navigate. In a storm the waters would boil between the rocks and throw a small boat to those jagged teeth.

From the beach a bastion of cliffs towered into the sky; birds nested and fluttered in their crevices, and flowering seaweeds trailed from rock crannies.

They tied up at a stone jetty, and Domini saw that the beach was scalloped into coves concealed from each other by water-silked boulders. Ribbon-weed curled on the pale sand like snakes and there were clumps of sea-holly and bush pine to provide shade from the glare of the sun and the sea.

Domini stood looking about her, wondering how on earth they reached the house from the beach. She soon found out! Their galley-boy came running towards them holding a large electric torch, which he handed to Paul with a flashing smile. Paul spoke to him in Greek, gesturing towards the boat and evidently giving an order concerning their baggage, then imperturbably he led Domini through the opening of a large cave.

"Long ago this was a hideout of smugglers," he told her. "It leads directly to the house and is perfectly safe. The tides are low here, rising only in exceptionally bad weather, when it is wiser to steer clear of the beach altogether."

"Well," Domini laughed, "what a novel way for a man to bring home his bride . . . but I must say in keeping with the pirate in you."

Her words echoed in the cave, as did his answering laughter. Domini glanced at him as they traversed the rocky tunnel, following the bright, guiding finger of the torch. Strange, unpredictable man, grinning like a boy —well, almost, his eyes no longer obscured by those enigmatic dark glasses but glimmering smoky-gold as he met her side glance.

"The ground is elevating, can you feel it?" he said. "Soon we will reach a door that opens on to steps that lead up to the garden. This secret passage has an appeal for you, no?"

"Yes," she agreed with a smile. "You know I'm an incurable romantic."

"It is in the British to be that way." He shrugged in his foreign way, and in a few more minutes the torch lit up an oval-shaped wooden door which swung open on a twisting flight of rough stone steps. "Please to go carefully," Paul warned. "They are crumbling away with age—now mind!" He caught hold of her as she stumbled, and for an instant in the half-light she was locked against his hard warmth—her breath caught in her throat, she thought he was going to kiss her, but he let her go and she preceded him up the steps, trying to look as though she wasn't hurrying.

He followed silently, out under an arbour of wild grape on to a pathway that led through a garden laid out in a series of rising terraces. Cypresses, both jade-green and golden, rose above clumps of wistaria and morning-glory. Oleanders hung their rose-bells in the sun, and there were cool green pepper-trees in which tiny bright birds flitted and flirted.

"At the other side of the house we overlook a pine forest," Paul said, bending to pluck a scented cluster of jasmine and tucking it casually into Domini's hair. The starry petals clung like confetti to her honey hair, their scent stealing rich to her nostrils. It was a pagan gesture, crowning her with a love-flower in this garden that seemed suspended above the sea. It was as though he said without words that tonight she would be alone with him in his house for the first time.

The house on the eagle's crag, isolated from the world, had a brooding air of mystery about it to the girl who had come there as a bride.

Its walls were a mellow-gold, and it had the clean

lines of a Greek temple, with more steps that led up to a wide *piazza* that was like an outdoor lounge. This was set round with tub chairs and loungers, elbow-level tables, and enormous stone pots in which gushed and bloomed a variety of trailing plants. From here, as Domini took a look over the parapet, there was a drop as bottomless as human folly, sheer to the sea and the rocks.

She drew back with a little gasp, then turned to face Paul as he spoke. "Come," he held out a brown hand to her, "let me show you the inside of the house."

She went to him, still unnerved by that dizzying drop, put her hand into his and was led into the house through a sliding glass door. "This is the *salotto*," he gestured round the big living-room, at the great curving settee and its matching armchairs, scrolled Venetian mirrors, carved cabinets, and the huge brass chandelier that was let down by a pulley so that the range of elaborate oil-lamps could be lit. Then it was raised again, old-fashioned but bound to appeal to someone of Domini's romantic disposition.

"You like the *tzaki*, no?" Paul indicated the vast stone fireplace, and the waiting pine logs in a wrought-iron basket. "Here in the evenings it grows cool and the British like the cosiness of a fire blazing up the chimney, is this not so?"

She shot a wide-eyed look at him. Suddenly he seemed more overwhelmingly foreign than ever. She nodded quickly in answer to his remark, and glanced away from him to the end of the room, where a semi-circle of dark-wood steps led to a platform on which stood a piano. It gleamed and shone darkly, and looked a beauty! Domini's eyes glistened. One of her favourite pastimes was the piano, and though professionally untaught she had a good musical ear. Her uncle had loved her to

75

play to him on their much-hammered piano at Fairdane.

"You like it, Domini?" Paul murmured.

She nodded, and longed to sit down on that padded bench, to put back the shining lid that hid a world in which she could always lose herself.

"It is yours," Paul said.

"Mine?" She turned to look at him with uncertain eyes.

"The instrument was despatched from Athens three weeks ago," he smiled. "That platform was originally used by my grandfather for his very imposing desk— this room, in fact, was then a study, but in my time it becomes the *salotto*. That chandelier I had removed from the hall, those cabinets were rescued from odd corners of the house and polished until their fine graining was revealed, those bearskin rugs reposed in the lumber-room in my stepmother's time—ah, but you are not interested in all that!"

"On the contrary, Paul." She touched his wrist half-shyly, feeling the crisp dark hairs in which his watch-strap was meshed. "The room is—perfect. Tell me, what are those words carved across the stone frieze of the *tzaki?*"

"You begin to say Greek words with a good, biting accent," he approved. "Those words?" He walked to the fireplace and she followed and watched him trace with a finger the cryptic Greek motto. "Defy the powers of darkness like Apollo," he translated, in a low, almost expressionless voice.

"Apollo was the god of light, of course," she murmured, and she thought of Paul's inability to face a strong light, or the raw gold of the Greek sun which he loved on his body. They had sunbathed a lot on a beach some miles out of Athens, where he had stretched out face down on the sand like a great tawny cat, stripped but for brief swim-trunks. A pagan worshipper of the

76

sun that thrust knives into his eyes unless he protected them behind smoked glass.

Domini knew this was connected with the injury he had once sustained — she knew not how — which had inflicted that fearful jag at his temple.

"When shall I meet your stepsister?" she asked, knowing from what he had let drop on this subject that he was extremely fond of the girl, though he had been unable to get along with her mother. His own mother had died when he was four years old and his brother a baby; his father had remarried some years later and Kara had been the result of that marriage. It had not been a happy one. When Paul's father had died suddenly of cardiac failure, he had been at the helm of his racing yacht in the Ionian Sea. His wife had been on board with him, and she had been drowned when the yacht had careened to destruction under the blind guidance of a dead hand.

Kara lived with Paul's aunt because business took him away from Andelos such a lot. Domini was already making plans in her mind to have the girl here for week-ends. She felt instinctively that they were going to be friends.

"We will go and see Kara and Aunt Sophula tomorrow," Paul said. "And now let us continue our tour of your new home, Madame Stephanos."

Her new home! Full of passages, unexpected doors, dark carved furniture, handwoven Greek rugs, and at last the room where she was to sleep.

The room directly adjoining was Paul's and their baggage having been brought up from the shore and installed in their rooms, he went in to collect his briefcase and reappeared briefly to say that he was going downstairs to work for an hour or two while Domini got acquainted with everything on her own.

"Thank you for the piano, Paul." She stood fingering the charming Venetian lamps on her dressing-table.

The rugs drowned his footfalls, but suddenly he was reflected tall and dark behind her in the mirror. Her fair head came to his heart, and he drew her against him with an arm encircling her waist. "Now our life together really begins, Domini," he murmured into her soft hair, where his cluster of jasmine still clung and breathed out its scent.

Their eyes met in the mirror, and the old confusion swept through Domini as she saw possession glint in his tawny eyes. His lips crushed the jasmine in her hair, moved down the side of her neck to the hollow of her shoulder under the thin silk of her blouse. His lips burned through the silk, and she felt the hunger in him . . .

"Kiss me, Domini," he ordered as her heart pounded. "Come, turn round and kiss me."

She obeyed like a mechanical doll and reached up to press her lips against his dark cheek.

"That will do—for now." He smiled as he let her go, and gestured round her room. "You like your sleeping bower?" he asked.

"It's very pretty," she said shakily.

"Cool flower-blue and gardenia-cream to match my Sabine." He grinned wickedly. "And now I leave you in peace—*adio!*"

The door closed behind him, and she slowly relaxed out of the tenseness he always induced in her when he touched her. She removed the jasmine from her hair and popped it out of sight in one of the nest-like drawers of the antique dressing-table. She then took up her hairbrush—someone had unpacked for her—and was brushing the jasmine petals from her hair when there was a tap on her door.

She swung round nervously and unable to think of the Greek words for, "Come in," she said it in English. Lita entered. She was smiling in her grave way and wished to know if there was any small service she could do for Domini.

"No, I can manage perfectly." Domini smiled in return, for it was a warm relief to see a face she knew in this house that was so strange as yet. "Thank you for asking, Lita."

"Until you acquire a maid, madame, I am available." Lita straightened the lace coverlet of the double bed and placed Domini's nightdress-case in a more exact position.

"Oh, I don't think I shall bother with a maid, Lita." Domini swept her hair into a pony-tail and secured it. "I'm used to managing on my own, and it seems so— decadent, somehow, being waited on hand and foot."

Lita looked rather taken aback by this outburst from her young mistress. "A reliable girl from the village would appreciate the employment, madame," she said. "Our girls are brought up to be handy and obedient, and to have a personal maid is the accepted thing for a lady in your position."

"*Malista, malista.*" Domini broke into a laugh. "Very good, very well, but if you're so determined to foist a maid on to me, then you can see to the matter. Really, you Greek people are the most determined, obstinate race—aren't you?"

"We are, madame." Lita was smiling again as she bent to pick up one by one the starry petals that lay like confetti on the soft rug in front of the dressing-table. Domini glanced down at the woman's smooth dark head, and she wondered if she would ever get used to the managing ways of the Greeks. Life at Fairdane had been so easy-going and uncomplicated. There had been no servant problem, for Domini had done most of the work of the rooms they used with the help of a daily woman.

"Did you enjoy your holiday with Yannis?" Domini asked, after Lita had swept her eagle eye round the room to ensure that all was now perfect to match the freshness of the gardenia-cream paint and the flower-blue curtains, padded bedhead, cushioned recliner, and little silk sewing chair.

"We helped with the work of his father's small farm at Sparta," Lita replied gently. "It was a labour of love and therefore a holiday in itself."

Domini stood thinking over Lita's words after she had gone. It was true; you did not begrudge a duty or a sacrifice if you gave out of love.

Then with a briskness that had the look of courage, she did as Paul had suggested and got acquainted with her new home. The interior of the house was rich with cypress and cedarwood. Age and hands had worn the carved stair-rails to a dark glossiness, while many feet had grooved the stairs. From a lyre-window at the bend of the massive, black-cedar staircase she saw a sea of pine trees. The afternoon was waning and a violet haze seemed to drift above the forest; the spicy scent of the pines had a sharpness to it, and she could hear the cicadas like a pulse-beat.

Domini went on down the stairs to the hall, feeling a lonely stranger in this big house that was cut off from the world, surrounded by the whispers of the ocean and the pines. She opened several doors and glanced into the rooms beyond them, but she was careful to avoid the one in which Paul was working. He had shown her his office on their way upstairs earlier on, and it was a relief to Domini to know that Paul would be spending part of each day at his desk.

While he was working she would be free . . . free to explore the island, to bathe in the Ionian Sea, and make friends with Kara. Pursuits that would surely help her to face up to the evenings and nights that would belong to Paul.

Yannis brought tea and cakes to her in the *salotto,* and after chatting to him for several minutes she wandered out on to the *piazza* to drink her tea by the parapet. From here the horizon arched like the silver bow of Apollo, shafting arrows of flame as the sun burned out. It was a pagan, breathtaking scene at which Domini caught her breath, then as dusk crept into the sky, she went indoors and made her way upstairs to bathe and dress for dinner.

Dinner was always a late affair in Greek households, so she had plenty of time for a lazy soak and a splash in a tub large enough to swim in. There was a hand-shower on a flexible tube and Domini stood up to direct a cool spray of water all over her.

She was tingling with the sybaritic pleasure of this pastime when to her utter consternation Paul strolled into the bathroom. Cool as a cat, he smiled at her as he unhooked a large towelling robe off the wall. Domini stood gaping at him like a startled naiad, with her honey hair swirled into a knot at the top of her head and only her blush to cover her. "Don't be all night, my dear," Paul said, and as he strolled out again his broad grin was reflected in the wall mirror beside the door.

"Well," Domini muttered to herself, "he might have knocked!"

Later, when she joined him for an aperitif in the *salotto,* she saw from the twinkle in his eye that he was still enjoying the joke. She caught his eyes as he handed her a fluted glass with sherry in it, and she knew what he was thinking—that she should not be shy with him when he already knew her every line and curve.

She took a quick, confused sip at her aperitif, and glanced away from him round the room. Topaz velvet curtains were drawn across the wide sweep of windows, fat pine logs purred in the fireplace, and there were pale gold flowers arranged in amber-glazed vases on the cabinets.

"I love the tangy smell of the resin in those logs," Domini murmured. "This entire room, in fact, is rather beautiful."

"A weakness of mine, Domini." He was smiling quizzically as he looked at her. "I have a Greek eye for beauty."

"Is that your only excuse, Paul?" she asked in a low voice, and her ringed hand had stolen to the chiffon swathing the throat of her sleeveless sheath.

"Not quite," he replied, catching her meaning at once.

"I had another reason, but I don't intend to tell you at this stage what it was."

Her heart seemed to pound beneath her fingers when he said that. What was he implying — that he had wanted her for his wife because he *loved* her?

CHAPTER SEVEN

"CHILD, will you be still?" implored the rather sad-eyed woman who sat making lace in a basket chair. She wore unrelieved black, from the snood covering her grey hair to the tips of her narrow shoes. The small radio standing on the table beside her chair showed that she had passed the first three years of deep mourning for her husband and could now enjoy some light entertainment.

"But, Aunt Sophula, they will be here any minute!" Kara Stephanos danced from one foot to the other, then hung precariously over the iron balustrade of the terrace. It directly overlooked the road that wound up from the harbour of Andelos, and she would see *their* car the moment it came into view. Her sunburned face was tense with excitement, and her aunt shook her head as she glanced up from her lacework. There were scratch marks on Kara's arms again where she had been at them with her fingernails. So unsightly! Paul would really have to agree to the child seeing a nerve specialist . . .

"Here they are—they are coming!" Kara flashed past her aunt's chair and leapt like a Pegasus down the steps that led to a side patio, across which she sped to a small door that opened on to the road. She couldn't get it open fast enough, her eyes shining as she raced to the cream car that was pulling to a standstill in front of the house.

"Welcome home, Paul!" she cried out in Greek, and he slid quickly out from behind the wheel, and Domini watched as he swept the slight figure of his sister up into his arms and they kissed with joyous, foreign abandonment. "Paul!" The girl cradled his face in her brown hands and her tears fell on to his cheek. "I have missed you so," she said huskily. "How have you been, my brother?"

"I have been fine, little one." Again he kissed her warmly. "Now, my squirrel, come and meet my wife Domini." He lowered Kara to her feet and led her to the car. He opened the passenger door and Domini stepped out on to the sun-hot flags fronting the house. She wore a sleeveless shantung dress in pale blue and she looked so cool and lovely that Paul's sister just stood gaping at her.

"Kiss your new sister, Kara." Paul spoke in English, and the girl stepped nervously towards Domini. "Welcome to Andelos and to our family, Domini," she said, flushing shyly as she felt the soft touch of Domini's lips against her brown cheek. Then she stepped back against Paul, and with a slight laugh he twined an arm about her boyish waist.

"How is everyone, Kara?" he asked. "Aunt Sophula keeps well?"

"Yes, but she has been very snappy with me." Kara twisted to look up at him. "I have bad nerves, she says, and she is going to ask you to send me to see a nerve specialist."

"What nonsense!" he exclaimed, though Domini saw him frown. "What have you been getting up to?"

"Well—sometimes I scratch." Kara was doing it as she spoke, reddening her left forearm with the rough-edged nails of her right hand. Paul frowned down at her and gave her hand a slap. Then he glanced up and said dryly to Domini: "Kara is not really a monkey, my dear. She merely acts like one."

Kara gave a shamed little laugh, then she drew one of her brother's hands to her lips and kissed it. She searched his face with her quick dark eyes. "I think you like being married, Paul," she said naively, and he responded to this by giving her tilt of a nose an affectionate tweak.

"You will make Domini blush with your remarks," he chuckled. "She is British, you must remember, and not yet used to our way of speaking from the heart."

"But I am so happy you are married and settled down, Paul," his sister said impetuously. Then she gave Domini her elfin smile. "I began to think he never would, and it is not good for a man to be without a wife. I am pleased until I could sing that my dear and only brother—" she paused and crossed herself in the Greek way, "has found for himself such a beautiful wife."

"Thank you, Kara." Domini felt rather humbled before the touching innocence and faith of this girl, and she grew afraid in her heart in case Kara should come to realise that her brother and his wife were less in love than she believed.

She watched Paul with his young sister, and she saw the flash of appeal in his eyes when as the three of them were about to enter the house, Kara suggested that he kiss Domini on the doorstep so that the blessing of their love would enter with them.

"Well, don't just stand looking at me, Paul," Domini laughed, and he took her in his arms, held her close against him and kissed her lips with unexpected tenderness.

They had come to spend a weekend at this old Greek mansion above the harbour of Andelos. His aunt had telephoned and insisted on it, and now here she was in the hall of her house, greeting her nephew and his bride with the grape jelly and iced water of Greek custom.

Kara then asked eagerly if she could show Domini to her bedroom. "Yes, yes, you fidget of a child!" Her aunt laid a hand on Paul's sleeve. "Come, nephew, you and I will talk on the terrace. I have some things to say—"

"Some of them about me, I bet!" Kara wrinkled her nose and caught at Domini's hand. Together they crossed the hall to a staircase with wrought-iron balustrade and went upstairs and along a gallery.

"Aunt Sophula despairs of making a lady of me," Kara laughed. "I was expelled from my school in Athens a few months ago, you know."

"Oh dear!" Domini cast a side glance at Kara. "Whatever for?"

"Playing my zither at a local *taverna*. It was fun, but the principal of my school said I was precocious and impudent, and when Paul came to collect me they had a fearful row. Paul knows that I do not mean to be wild —I am not really wild."

"You're at the mixed-up stage?" Domini suggested.

"Exactly so! I am half a child, and half a woman, and rebelling against being both. Ah, I knew you would understand." Domini's hand received a squeeze. "I saw it in your eyes right away — this is your room and Paul's."

As Kara threw open the door of an old-fashioned double room, Domini felt a pulse flutter in her throat. Her weekend case had been brought upstairs with Paul's; the maid had unpacked them and laid her chiffon wisp of a nightdress close beside his dark silk pyjamas.

Kara went over and bounced on the big carved bed. "Yes, you will both be comfortable in this," she announced, and she touched Domini's night wear with shy fingers. "Are you not cold in this cobweb—ah, but of course not!" She gave a laugh and gazed with innocent pleasure at Domini. "Perhaps after all it is good to be a woman, no?"

"It has its joys and tears," Domini agreed dryly, and she tossed into Kara's lap a small package she had taken out of her handbag.

"Now what is this?" Kara murmured, and was smilingly told to unwrap it and see. Kara did so with excited fingers and caught her breath as she lifted the lid of the square box and exposed a wafer-thin compact with an embroidered egret on the front. There was also a lipstick case with the same motif. Kara gazed at her sunburned scrap of a face in the compact mirror and grinned. "I wish I was pretty to match your gift, Domini," she said. *"Efharisto* many times over."

"Parakalo," Domini smiled.

Kara stroked the egret on her compact, then she said, "What does it feel like to be beautiful—really beautiful, as you are?"

Domini's smile faded and she gazed at Paul's sister in a rather stricken way. The truth was too stark; she could not reply: "I've learned that beauty is a snare. I hate it, for it has made me your brother's possession, and because I am his mere possession I am driven to hurt him. I can't stop hurting him. I've become cruel and small because I have this face—this body!"

"Beauty is only skin deep," she said stiffly.

"Meaning that you might not be beautiful under your skin?" Kara's glance was speculative. She, who was young in some of her ways, was older in others, and Domini tautened there at the foot of the bed in case Kara should sense her lack of love for Paul.

"Paul wrote to tell me that you were like a Medici painting," Kara said. "I thought he must be exaggerating."

"A-a what?" Domini stammered.

"A Medici painting. And now I see that he was not exaggerating. You do have the cool, patrician glamour of a Medici—and I expect Barry Sothern will want to paint you. Barry lives in a cottage on the beach—my aunt calls him a scamp, but all the same he is brilliant. He also is English, like you, Domini."

Domini had gone as white as a sheet. Barry was *here* —here in Greece, living in a cottage on the island of Andelos! She swayed, and Kara scrambled off the bed and came quickly to her. "What is the matter, *kyria*?" The girl put an arm around her. "Are you faint?"

Domini pulled herself together. "It's probably the heat," she said shakily. "I-I haven't quite got used to your Greek sunshine."

"You will feel better when you have had a cup of tea." Kara gazed with concern at Domini's pale face. "Shall I have tea brought here, or would you prefer to join the others on the terrace?"

"Let's go to the terrace." Domini felt in need of some air after the shock of learning that Paul—of all people — had brought her to the one place where Barry was. It was like destiny, she thought, as she went to the mirror to comb her hair. But there, as she gazed into her own wide eyes, she saw that she was afraid as well as eager to see Barry.

She was afraid of Paul, who had reminded her only the other day that honour was included in the vows she had made when she became his wife.

She was retouching her mouth with rose lipstick when knuckles rapped the door and Paul strolled into the room, one hand in the pocket of the light slacks he wore with a sand-coloured sports shirt. "Don't you two girls want any refreshments?" he asked. "Tea is now being laid on the terrace."

"I'm just tidying up, Paul." Domini hoped that his sister wouldn't mention her weakness of a minute ago, and she watched in the mirror as he bent over Kara and cradled her face in his hands. "Why the pensive expression, little one?" he smiled. "I thought you were pleased to see your brother home again. You were most generous with your kisses when we met in the forecourt by the car."

Kara gazed up at him and lifted a hand to his black hair and his scarred temple. She spoke to him in Greek, and Domini, who was beginning to pick up a little of the language from Paul, was fairly certain that Kara said something about his headaches.

Domini could not make out his reply, but his tone of voice was light, and he added in English: "Well, Kara, what did you think of the present I sent you from Athens?"

The girl's face lit up. Domini knew from Paul that his sister had a passion for folk music; she collected old songs, mainly Greek, as other girls might collect baubles or boys. She had stacks of music in her room, and she could play several musical instruments. Paul had discovered a really lovely mandolin in a shop tucked away in the Plaka and had had it sent to Kara.

"It has a gorgeous lilting tone," Kara enthused. "I will play it for you and Domini after dinner tonight. It is an instrument to be played under the stars."

"We will look forward to that," he smiled. "Domini is musical herself. She plays the piano extremely well."

"Domini likes music?" Kara's eyes were sparkling like black diamonds. "Oh, the Fates are being so good to me today. Domini is as nice as she is beautiful — and she plays the piano!" Kara gave her brother a hug. "Thank you for my mandolin and for my sister-in-law, big brother."

"I am happy they both please you." A grin slashed his brown cheek as he glanced at Domini. "Are you ready, my dear?"

She nodded, cool and composed again, a smile in her eyes for Kara's youthful enthusiasm. How blissfully fond of Paul she was, and amusingly wasp-like in her striped amber shirt and black play-pants, with the warm, frank gaze of a child. She had never been face to face with the tyrant in Paul, and Domini envied her.

Up on the terrace the Venetian-like aspect of Andelos harbour was unrolled before Domini like a colourful tapestry, and she stood at the balustrade with Paul and Kara as they directed her attention to the fishing caiques with their painted sails, and the white stone convent with purple bougainvillaea trailing over its walls. To smaller, nearby islands set in the blue Ionian like brilliant clumps of coralline.

Domini gazed around her with interest, while the sun shone brightly on her hair and her shantung dress clung softly to her slender body, which always assumed a look of fragility when close to the power and strength of her husband's.

She was unaware that she was being stared at by the man who lounged in a basket chair adjacent to the one in which Paul's aunt was sitting. It was Kara who caught his stare as she turned in her quick way from the balustrade. "Hullo!" she exclaimed. "I had no idea you were coming to tea, *kyrie*."

"I wanted to help lay out the 'welcome home' mat," he replied, and at the sound of his voice Domini went very still, then slowly she turned around . . . and found herself face to face with Barry Sothern again! He had hardly changed at all, except for the slight touches of increased prosperity. His lazy sorrel eyes gazed straight into hers, and she remembered so well that wide, gay mouth and crooked smile — that mane of lion-gold hair!

She wondered wildly if he would admit to knowing her, then feminine instinct told her that he wouldn't, and the knowledge both excited and troubled her as he rose loose-jointedly out of his chair and said to Paul: "You certainly have the luck of Apollo, old man." His smile was ironical. "If you fell in the sea, I bet you'd come up with an oyster in your ear — an oyster with a pearl in it!"

"I can see, my friend, by the gleam in your artistic eye that my 'pearl' appeals to you." And as Paul escorted Domini to the terrace table and introduced Barry to her, she felt the possessive clasp of his arm about her waist.

"Kara informs me that your work is quite brilliant, Mr. Sothern," Domini said, knowing from the moment she accepted Barry as a stranger that she was playing a rather dangerous game.

"I'll be happy to show you some of my work one of these days—Domini," he replied, little glints in his sorrel eyes.

Beware! warned her heart, as she saw Paul slant one of his keen looks at Barry. And yet at the same time she wanted to say: *"I knew this man long before you walked into my life, my handsome tyrant. He came with laughter, not with threats, and he went away because I was so young when we met and he had to find his footing as a painter."*

"I shall look forward to seeing some of your work, Mr. Sothern," she said. "I should imagine that the crystal quality of the light here in Greece must be marvellous for an artist to work by. Colours and lines must take on an added enchantment."

"They certainly do—Madame Stephanos." He bore down meaningly on the name, and his eyes raked the delicate symmetry of her face framed in the sunlit honey hair. Her eyes were a cool, still blue, and Barry, who remembered so well their sparkling gaiety, was disturbed as he watched her take a chair beside Paul's aunt. She answered questions about her wedding and her honeymoon as Aunt Sophula poured tea from a fluted pot. Kara handed round cakes and fruit, and finally perched herself on the arm of her brother's chair, her small teeth nibbling at a large fig.

"I take it you visited the Acropolis while you were in Athens?" Barry remarked.

"Both in daylight and in the evening," Domini replied. "I liked it with the cicadas hidden in the trees, and the Temples of Jupiter and Victory cloaked in the violet dusk."

"Domini is one of those women who prefers the masked to the unveiled," Paul said with a dry smile. "Those scarred columns worried her in the broad light of day."

"Most women are romantic," Barry said, and he was looking at Domini as he bit into a cake. "I wonder, Monsieur Stephanos, if you will permit me to paint your wife? I see her as Britomartis, the virgin goddess."

Domini flushed when Barry said that, for all eyes were upon her—Paul's unreadable behind the smoked lenses of his sunglasses. *"Don't, Barry,"* she wanted to say. *"Don't make things harder than they are for me."*

"What a lovely idea!" Kara smiled across innocently at Domini, then she looked at Paul. "You must let Barry paint Domini," she urged excitedly. "Ooh, that will make Alexis jealous. She thinks there is no one as attractive as she."

"Where is Alexis, by the way?" Paul asked, with a hard look to his mouth that told Domini he had not liked Barry's request. Alexis, his sister-in-law, provided a handy change of topic.

"She has gone sailing with some people who have taken a house nearby," Kara told him. "They are staying for the summer. They are rich Americans, so Alexis is cultivating them—naturally."

"That will be enough, Kara!" her aunt put in sharply. "It is Alexis' own business if she prefers civilised company to that of fisherfolk and beachcombers."

"I think Aunt Sophula is referring to you, Barry, because you have a beach cottage," Kara laughed, her glance dwelling on his bare, tanned feet in Roman-type sandals.

He nonchalantly crossed his legs and brushed crumbs from his slacks. Domini knew from his grin that he was thinking of the old days, his lion-mane of hair to the rolled collar of his fisher-jersey and the turn-ups of his paint-splashed slacks above sandals that had not been hand-tailored. One evening on an upturned boat on that English beach he had hinted that he must go away . . . his lips had brushed her cheek, and yet she had not felt sad, for she had known they would meet again . . .

There Domini tore her thoughts away, and when she looked at Paul she saw that Kara had curled down into his arms like a kitten. His aunt shook her grey head in its black snood as she regarded the pair of them. "Paul, you are spoiling her," she reproved. "Kara is almost seventeen and must begin to learn a little restraint. You treat her like a kitten, and not all men like their women to make of them the comfortable armchair."

Laughter ran like a wave to Paul's mouth and he smoothed his young sister's seal-dark hair. It was oddly cut, as though she might have been having a go at it with the scissors. "Ah well," Paul smiled, "we have not seen each other for almost three months and I owe her a little pampering."

Kara blinked her tilting dark eyes and she seemed almost to be purring as she rubbed her cheek against his sports shirt. That deep note of indulgence in his voice caused Domini to remember—almost too vividly—the night she had lain in his arms at the Cornish villa where they had started their honeymoon. That deep, warm voice had lured her into a fool's paradise . . . how it had hurt, how it still hurt, finding out that Paul had tricked her.

"How strange that I must now think of Paul as the husband of another girl," Kara smiled across at Domini.

"I hope you don't mind that I use your husband as an armchair?"

"You're welcome to him," Domini said lightly, and she didn't miss the narrowing of Paul's eyes, or the long look that Barry gave his wristwatch . . . as though he had detected something in her manner that caused a flare in his eyes that had to be hidden until he had controlled it. Her pulses raced as she felt the danger in the atmosphere.

"Thank you for tea, Madame Stephanos." Barry rose to his feet and gave Paul's aunt a polite bow. Then he glanced at Domini. "I hope you'll enjoy life on the island. Perhaps you and Kara will call on me one of these days."

"That would be nice." And to tease him, Domini added: "I'll think about it."

"And will you think about letting me paint your wife, Monsieur Stephanos?" Barry's glance swung to Paul.

Domini felt that Barry's question was a challenge and she waited with bated breath for Paul's reply. "Yes, you may paint my wife, Mr. Sothern," he said, "but not yet. I take it you will not mind waiting a few months?"

"I take it that I *must* wait?" Barry gave a shrug and a laugh. "It's a good thing I've taken a year's lease on the cottage."

"I shall not keep either of you waiting a year," Paul drawled, and at the side of her Domini heard his aunt catch her breath as her lace-needle jabbed her finger.

"Clumsy—so clumsy in my old age," she muttered, meeting Domini's side glance. "There, I have marked the lace!"

"What a shame." Domini spoke with automatic politeness, her eyes following Barry as he strolled to the terrace steps, tall, loose-jointed, the sun on the raw gold of his hair. Even yet Domini could hardly believe that Barry was back in her life . . . but as a stranger, someone she must treat distantly when she longed to run her fingers through that crisp mane of hair, and to say his name openly, Barry, so gay and British . . .

"Don't forget our party for Domini and Paul tomorrow evening," Kara called out after him. "You will be coming, *kyrie?*"

"Nothing could keep me away." He smiled round at her from the steps. "*Adio,* everyone, until tomorrow night."

There was a dull sort of silence after he had gone, then Kara slipped out of her brother's lap and asked Domini if she would like to see the frock she would be wearing for the party. Domini welcomed the chance to get away, but as she passed her husband's chair he caught her hand and detained her for a moment. She felt her heart beating in her throat as he scrutinised her face from behind the smoked lenses that made him look so enigmatic—and unnerving.

"You seemed to find Barry Sothern an interesting person," he said quietly.

"I suppose that's because he's British," she replied, and she was conscious of the tightening of Paul's fingers.

"One of your own kind, eh, Domini?" A smile came and went on Paul's chiselled mouth. "Do you still feel such a stranger with me?"

She bit her lip and felt Kara and his aunt looking at them, then Paul deliberately turned her hand palm upwards and kissed it. Domini bore the kiss without any warmth at her heart, knowing it to be a seal on his possession—his caprice.

The touch of his lips lingered . . . lingered as she went down the terrace steps with Kara.

CHAPTER EIGHT

DOMINI gave a gasp of mingled amusement and shock, for Kara's apartment resembled a junk shop dealing in odd musical instruments and illustrated sheet music. Kara grinned at Domini's expression and picked up the ribboned mandolin which her brother had given her. She ran a thin hand over its grained and gleaming pear-shape, and watched with gipsy-dark eyes as Domini paused before the bureau on which stood several framed photographs.

Domini picked up a photograph of a lovely brunette wearing a foreign-looking wedding-gown and headdress. Kara came and peered over her shoulder. "That was Paul's mother," she said. "Paul resembles her, do you not think? That is our father in the companion frame. Poor Papa, he was not so happy with *my* mother. I don't remember her too well. Aunt Sophula always says of her that she was the foolish whim of a man of middle years."

Kara plucked a little tune out of her *bouzouki*. "I am the odd result of their union," she laughed.

"Who says you're odd?" Domini was nettled on the girl's behalf, for there was a piquancy about her that Domini liked; an elfin quality that was innocent and touching.

"Oh—Alexis," Kara shrugged. "Sometimes my aunt. They don't understand me, and think it odd that I should like folk music so much."

"Alexis was married to your younger brother, wasn't she, Kara?" Domini was beginning not to like the sound of Paul's sister-in-law.

"Yes, she was wife to Loukas." A cloud passed over Kara's face. "He died eighteen months ago—at sea like Papa. The sea is cruel to us, though we take our living from it."

"I'm sorry about your brother, Kara." Domini spoke gently, and glimpsing tears in the girl's eyes she turned her attention to another photograph in order not to embarrass her. The dark, framed face stared back at her —Paul when he had been about Kara's age, but a Paul who bewildered her, for he was clad so oddly in a sheepskin tunic and a wool cap worn at a rakish angle above his thin young face.

"Paul was only sixteen when he fought in the rebellion," Kara said proudly. "He was an *andarte,* a guerilla fighter. He was badly hurt by a grenade during the fighting in Athens and he—he almost died. That is how he got the scar." Kara touched a finger to his unscarred face in the photograph. "The scar does not matter. Paul is still the handsomest man on the island, and you and he will have such lovely children—"

There she broke off as Domini replaced the photograph on the bureau in such a hurry that it fell over and had to be set right. "Really, Kara," Domini gave a brittle little laugh, "your brother and I have been married only a few weeks. W-we aren't thinking of starting a family just yet."

"But babies are such fun," Kara said warmly. "They are the nicest part of being married—or so it seems to me."

"I-I don't want to talk about it, if you don't mind, Kara." Domini was trembling slightly as she turned the pages of a book of sea-shanties, but Kara, looking rather bewildered, pursued the subject with half-childish persistence.

"Don't you wish to give Paul a child?" she asked.

"The pride of all Greek women is to give their man a son. Are English women so different? Are they cold—like their beauty?"

"We—just aren't in the habit of discussing so private a matter," Domini replied, in a low, shaken voice. She was far from indifferent to children; they were cute and affectionate and absorbing at all stages of their growth —but a child should be born out of love, and it wasn't love that Paul felt when he took her in his arms.

"Do we, and the island, seem strange to you?" Kara plonked a mandolin string, and quizzed the cameo coolness of Domini's face in profile, its fine-drawn tension as she pretended to study the book in her hands.

"Andelos is another world to me," Domini admitted. "I feel the pull of its fable-like atmosphere, and yet at the same time I am aware of—of not belonging."

"But of course you belong," Kara protested. "You are Paul's wife, and that makes you one of us. No doubt our ways will seem strange to you at first, but in no time at all you will be feeling and acting as the wife of a Greek —and loving it," Kara added with a laugh. "Paul is very masterful, of course, and you are very British, and it is only natural that you fight a little. But as we say in Greece, what is a marriage without the relish of fighting and making up?"

"Is that how it looks, Kara, that we fight?" Domini asked quietly.

"I would say there is some conflict between you," Kara agreed. "But the beginning of marriage is a time of adjustment, and happiness has to be earned, not handed to us on a plate."

"Are all Greek people so philosophical?" Domini smiled.

"Of course." In her play-clothes, cradling her *bouzouki* with its gay ribbons, Kara looked like a win-

98

some gnome as she gazed back at Domini. "The Greeks were civilised when others were barbarians, you know."

The girl bent her dark head and strange Greek music rippled out of the stringed instrument that had been born out of those played in the Ionic temples of long ago. Domini listened and thought of Paul, and the tiger that roamed under that well-groomed veneer of his.

Tiger, tiger . . . purring in the dark, smoky-gold eyes drowsy from the passion she aroused in him, and hated. She stood very still, her eyes on that youthful photograph of him.

"You play well, Kara," she said as the music died away.

"This is an instrument to make any music sound good." Kara stroked the mandolin with loving fingers. "Paul always gives me presents I love. Once when he returned from a trip he brought me a real rose-bush with toy singing birds attached to the branches. But that was when I was younger."

Domini smiled, and when she left Kara to go to her room—and Paul's—the strange Greek music followed her.

She opened the door of the big double room, and stiffened when she walked in and saw Paul out on the balcony. He turned upon hearing her, and strolled in to join her, a cheroot held in long fingers. "Do you like this old mansion above the harbour?" he asked with a smile.

She walked into the centre of the room, and he saw the hard shine of her eyes, as though iced tears lay in them. "What do you want me to reply, Paul, that the place is charming and I shall love visiting here?" With a tired, rather lost gesture, she pushed the burnished hair back from her eyes. "The house is charming, but it's full

99

of your relations and they're bound to guess how matters stand between us. Do you know what Kara has just been talking about?"

"I cannot begin to guess," he drawled, lifting his cheroot and drawing on it, the smoke rising blue about his smoky-gold eyes.

"She was talking about children," Domini flung at him, *"ours."*

"I am sorry Kara upset you." His eyes hardened as they scanned her scornful face. "But she is little more than a child herself and so she says what is in her heart. You must not take her remarks so seriously."

"Would you suggest that I apply your advice to the rest of this—situation?" Domini demanded. "This pretence that we're happy newlyweds with not a cloud on our horizon?"

"Greek people are not demonstrative in public and my relations would be offended rather than otherwise if you hung over me," he smiled thinly, "and showed your affection—that is if you had any for me—openly."

"It's one relief to know that I needn't act the starry-eyed bride." Domini gave a hard little laugh. "I was never any good at pretending, not even as a child. If someone told me there were elves in the woods, then I believed them."

"What of unicorns, Domini?" He lifted his cheroot with lazy composure and smiled through the smoke. "Do you recall the one you bought for me with all the money you had, clutching it in your hand like a child as you ran to give it to me?"

"Oh, I was a child all right," Domini said coldly. "A little fool who sang for a few hours like—like a blinded bird."

"Ah—" the smile was flicked off his face as though by acid. "You are learning how to be cruel, Domini."

"I have the best of teachers," she threw the words over her shoulder as she took lingerie out of a drawer and swung a long dress out of the wardrobe. "You, Paul."

She went into the small adjoining bathroom and as she closed the door behind her, she felt elation at having hurt him. That unicorn! It stood on his desk in that sombre office at the house on the eagle's crag, incongruous with its little twisted horn beside a big ebony inkstand. Paul seemed to reap a perverse satisfaction out of that symbol of her surrender—her total surrender—to him, but never again would that happen. She meant what she had said to him at the villa; he was welcome to what he had bought, but her heart was her own.

As she stepped from under the shower, she caught sight of her reflection in a mirror on the wall. Her eyes were those of a stranger, and with a towel draped around her she gazed in a quiet panic at herself. Where was Domini Dane, who as a child had searched for elves in the folded petals of windflowers, and who at seventeen had dreamed of a tall young man with gay eyes and a mane of lion-gold hair. Domini closed her eyes to shut out the girl in the mirror; the girl who belonged to a man she didn't love.

Domini had soon discovered that Greeks prefer to dine out of doors, under sunlight or starlight, and their *vradi,* or evening meal, begins late. They linger over it and talk of many things, and often it is midnight before they go to bed.

The stars were out when Domini walked with Paul across the dining courtyard to the table that caught a slanting light from wall lanterns. She wore apricot lace, and her fair hair framed her face in a casual style. Paul in dark evening wear seemed extra tall at her side. The dark suit and his distant manner intensified the impression, making of Domini a fragile focus for the eyes of a young woman who stood holding a cocktail beside an illuminated fountain. She wore a deep-necked dress in nectarine, and the subtle lights of the fountain showed off her dramatic cheekbones, her secret bayou eyes and the rich coil of dark-hair at the nape of her neck. With the poised walk of a woman who knows she is extremely attractive, she came towards Paul and Domini, who had guessed already that this was Alexis, the widow of Loukas who had been drowned eighteen months ago.

Paul introduced them, and Alexis studied Domini with cool deliberation as she asked how she was liking Andelos. Her English was very good, and her throat seemed full of cream as she spoke; deep, smooth, sensuous.

"I hope you will not find yourself too cut off from civilisation in that house of Paul's?" she drawled, while he turned to the table to pour a couple of aperitifs. His aunt and Kara had not yet appeared.

"I'm used to living in a country house," Domini replied, thanking Paul in an aside as she took her aperitif from him. She had not expected to like Alexis very much, and was confirmed in her feeling that she would find her the type who lived for herself alone. It hung about her like the ambergris perfume she wore; was as manifest as it is in a sleek and luxury-loving Persian cat.

"That house!" Her laugh matched her seductive body. "Paul, have I not said before it is like a fastness— a retreat?"

"You have," he agreed, taking a sip at his drink and meeting her eyes. "But it was built so that a man might find escape from the inanities of so-called civilisation."

"But Domini is a woman," those faintly wicked eyes

scanned the slender figure at his side, "and someone so pretty is certain to grow bored with being tucked away in that lonely retreat of yours. I know *I* should."

"You are a restless city creature, Alexis," he half smiled. "Domini is a country girl who, I am hopeful, will appreciate the sea and the pine trees whispering together at night, our hidden beach, and walking in the woods."

"Really?" Alexis gazed over the rim of her cocktail glass at Domini, who had never felt such a flare of antagonism towards another girl. Alexis wasn't in the least concerned that the house on the eagle's crag might prove lonely for Paul's wife; she was, Domini knew, a beautiful cat who had to rip into everything just for the fun of feeling her claws.

"I know I shall love the woods," Domini said. "They will remind me of—home."

"Do not let the wood-witch lure you too far into them, *kyria*," Alexis smiled narrowly. "You might get lost."

"I have known those woods from a boy," Paul said dryly. "If Domini goes astray, then I shall soon find her and bring her home."

"How masterful of you, Paul." Alexis gave him a slumbrous smile through her lashes. Then she looked at Domini. "Is it thrilling, or otherwise, for an Anglitha to be married to one of our possessive Greeks?"

Domini tensed beside Paul, and it was with relief that she saw Alexis turn her attention to the arrival of their hostess and a couple of menservants carrying trays of food. Kara appeared breathlessly, more elfin than ever in green, bringing her mandolin which she placed carefully on a lounger under some trees. "Are we going to be entertained when we have eaten?" Alexis drawled.

Kara shot a gipsy-dark glance at her sister-in-law.

"Domini wishes to hear some Greek music," she said. "Do you mind?"

"Who am I in this house to mind anything?" Alexis flicked her eyes over the younger girl. "Lipstick, Kara? Have you put it on for Nikos—ah, here he comes! Nikki, your little cousin has gone all sophisticated and is wearing lipstick in your honour."

Nikos, a slender, good-looking young Greek, ungallantly pulled Kara's hair as he passed her by and went straight to Paul to be introduced to the bride, as he put it. Shyness was obviously a stranger to him; he had all the charm of the young Adonis he looked, and Domini could tell that his widowed mother was extremely proud of him. Little Kara, she suspected, was smitten with him without fully knowing it, for she had blushed deeply at Alexis' mocking remarks and scrubbed the lipstick from her mouth with her handkerchief.

Nikos was placed beside Domini at the table, and his friendly conversation helped her to relax and enjoy the various Greek dishes; the soup with its tang of eggs and lemon, quails simmered in wine and served with a piquant dressing, and salad served from a huge cedar-wood bowl. Nikos, son of the house, did the mixing honours at the table, quoting with his gay smile: "A spendthrift for oil, a miser for vinegar, a counsellor for salt, and a lunatic to mix it."

Everyone laughed, and Domini, catching Paul's eye, realised that Nikos was like him as he looked in that photograph of him as a youthful guerrilla fighter. Since then a devil had entered in and the idealistic boy had changed into a man capable of utter ruthlessness. Did no one at the table suspect it? Or did they know and accepted it as natural in an adult Greek?

"Andelos must seem strange to you after England," Nikos remarked, a small glass of iced and cloudy *ouzo* held in his hand. "You must feel very far from the scents and sounds of your homeland?"

"Yes, England does feel a long way away," Domini agreed, and as though to endorse her words, a mocking-bird tinkled into song from its hiding place among the trees.

"Then Kara and I must do our best to help you feel at home, eh, little cousin?" Nikos winked across the table at Kara, who responded by pulling a face at him and smiling at Domini. He went on: "We will come to your house and take you swimming with us at night. It is like bathing in purple wine, and the stars are like bubbles in the wine."

"Sounds very exciting," Domini smiled, for this young man was quite irresistible. "What do we do after our swim, lie on the sand and get a moon-tan?"

He laughed aloud. "Paul, you must guard well this ice-daisy of yours, or I shall steal her," he said. "Are there many more like her in England?"

"You may go there on business for me some time," Paul smiled, "then you will see for yourself. I don't think, however, that you will find another quite like Domini."

"You always were the lucky one when it came to finding something unique," Nikos said admiringly. "I recall that carving of Andromeda on her rock." He glanced mischievously at Domini. "Paul always swore that he would not marry until he found a real-life Andromeda. I asked him what he would do if she belonged to someone else, or if she would not marry him, and do you know what he said?"

"I think I can guess." Her head was half bent, so that the lantern light played over a bright wing of her hair. "He said he would take her and pay the price . . . whatever it was."

"Ah, you know him well, Domini!" Nikos thumped the table in his delight—thinking this a game—and his mother reproved him for rattling the dishes and crockery.

"If you behave like a boy," she said, "Paul will think you are not yet ready for a position of importance in the business."

"Nikos is in high spirits, Aunt Sophula," Paul said lazily. "And I enjoy listening to the fancies which the young are full of."

"Come, Paul," the long lashes of Alexis stirred out of the cream of her cheeks and the look she slanted at him was full of secret laughter, "you are not yet in your dotage. You have your fancies, too."

Domini's fingers gripped the stem of her wine glass, for it seemed to her that Alexis, with cat-like perception, had guessed it was fancy, not affection, that had led Paul into marriage. Paul, the rich and attractive brother-in-law Alexis might well have fancied herself!

"I love all those old tales of fancy and fable," Kara said dreamily. "Paul's house always seems to me to have a mythical-castle look, perched on its crag high above the sea."

"And do you visualise Domini as the captive princess?" Nikos mocked affectionately.

Kara rested her elbow on the table and cupped her pointed chin in her hand. "Domini," she smiled, "is more like the swan-maid who discarded her disguise to bathe as a girl, and who was compelled to marry the man who stole her swansdown dress."

"What are you talking about, child?" Aunt Sophula shot an irritated glance at her niece. "You see, Paul! She lives in a world of make-believe."

"Kara is but sixteen—a child." He tossed back his *ouzo,* and Domini caught the glint of his eyes and knew he was angry. His young stepsister was probably the only person who had his complete affection, and Domini wondered if he would like her to live with them. It was fairly obvious that Kara was not all that happy in the keeping of her aunt, for behind his teasing manner Nikos could be showing her more attention than his mother liked. Also there was Alexis, whose sense of fun was neither as pleasant nor as innocent as the boy's.

Domini decided, then and there, to suggest to Paul that Kara be invited to spend some time with them. Her stay could be extended into a permanent arrangement if it turned out a happy one, and Domini felt certain that it would be. Kara was lively, musical, and Paul's house needed the scamper of young feet up and down its stairs, and laughter to wake it up. It had not been lived in enough in the past few years.

It was at this point that Domini came out of her reverie to find Alexis staring hard at her, taking in the little smile that half-parted her lips . . . lips shaped to receive kisses. Then Alexis glanced at Paul, and Domini saw the tightening of her full red mouth as her eyes measured the breadth of his shoulders, lifting to cling darkly to the lips that were stamped with decision, temper, and passion.

When everyone rose from the table to take coffee on the loungers under the trees, Domini was aware that Alexis was watching as Paul adjusted a lacy stole about her shoulders, and brushed from her honey hair a tiny moth. Though so light a touch, it was one of ownership for all the world to see . . . from her fair head to her small feet in silver kid shoes the cool and slender English girl was the possession of her imperious Greek husband.

And Alexis tensed as he led Domini to one of the more secluded loungers.

CHAPTER NINE

DOMINI had heard *bouzouki* music played in the *tavernas* of Athens, but it had been curiously unmusical in comparison to the fey magic which Kara enticed out of the instrument.

The courtyard flowers were asleep and dewed, exuding scents that Domini drew deep within her, along with the aromatic flavour of her Turkish coffee. The fretted lanterns lent mystery, romance, illusion . . . a spellbound night, made more so because the intoxication of seeing Barry again was haunting Domini's veins.

Kara was singing softly, partly in Greek, then in English. The words were strangely beautiful, those of a sonnet set to music, and a tremor ran through Domini as the song came to a sad ending.

> 'I cannot die if thou be not near,
> O spirit-face, O angel, with thy breath
> K   me to death!'

"Are you cold?" Paul's arm came close and hard around her.

"No, it's the music, that sad little song," she whispered, feeling as though the finger of destiny had stolen out of the night to quicken her heart under Paul's hand. The fountain sobbed into its stone basin, and the spell of the song was abruptly shattered by Alexis.

She rose to her feet and swept the circle of listeners with strangely brilliant eyes. "Let us all drive down to the Venetian Mask for some dancing," she suggested. "It will be fun—much livelier than sitting here listening to Kara's melancholy music. The Vanhusens are bound to be there. Barry Sothern might have dropped in. He likes to dance."

"Alexis, you are so energetic," Nikos said lazily, long legs stretched across the flags of the courtyard. "*I* like Kara's music."

"Oh, come on," Alexis said impatiently, looking as though she might stamp a high-heeled slipper if thwarted. "There is time enough to sit and listen to music when one is old. Right now I prefer to dance to it, and the Venetian Mask orchestra is a really good one."

"I should rather like to go." Domini's heart had given an excited little bound when Alexis had said that Barry might have dropped in at the club.

"Very well, we will go, if you are not too tired," Paul said obligingly.

"Does one ever grow tired in Greece?" With a sudden surge of gaiety Domini escaped out of his encircling arms, and went indoors with the other two girls to tidy her hair and get a warmer wrap.

Aunt Sophula declined to join the party, declaring that she was long past the age when it was more fun to dance than to sit at home with her memories. "You will see us at the break of dawn, little mother," Nikos laughed, and bent to kiss her cheek. She held his shoulders a moment and looked hungrily at him, then she let him go and he hustled his gamin-eyed cousin into a low-slung car. Alexis was about to slip into Paul's but Nikos caught her around the waist and said teasingly: "You will drive down with us, Alexis. Paul and Domini are still at the stage when they want to be alone."

"We shall be crushed in this buggy," Alexis said freezingly.

"Get in, woman," Nikos gave her a slight push, then

109

turned to shoot a smile at Paul. "We will drive ahead of you, cousin. The stars are low enough tonight to be kissed."

"They're gorgeous," Domini said, as Paul headed the cream car down the incline that dropped dizzyingly towards the harbour. "I didn't know stars could look so enormous—I could almost pluck one for myself."

"Do you think you are going to like living on the island?" Paul asked.

Domini breathed the scented maquis growing over the hills, and she could not deny her response to the fable-like beauty of Andelos. "Yes, the island is bewitching, Paul," she smiled, "Very much a place of 'eagles and dragons, wines of two kinds and spices.' "

He took a quick look into her eyes . . . blue as the Greek sea, and alight with an eagerness that brought a quizzical look to his face. Her heart turned over, for he must never guess that Barry's presence on the island made its sunshine that much brighter for her. The memory of how merciless he could be drove the pink flush out of her cheeks, and she went weak at the touch of his strong, taut body as the car rounded a steep bend.

"Paul," she said, her fingers clenching over her embroidered bag, "I've been thinking that it would be nice if Kara came to stay with us for a while. I-I'm sure she would enjoy it. She's so very attached to you, and I find her a delightful person."

He didn't answer for several moments, then he said: "I know you like Kara, but I think you are more afraid to be alone with me."

"You weren't thinking of making a total captive of me, up there on your crag, were you, Paul?" she asked, and felt him glance sharply at her. She sat up very straight beside him, her wrap draping her shoulders, and his ruby and pearl hearts gleaming against her earlobes.

"Darling, do you have to talk so dramatically?" he drawled, bringing to the endearment a caressing, foreign inflection that roused her to a sudden flash of anger.

"Pretend in front of other people that you're the fond husband, Paul," she flashed, "but don't do it when we're alone. Let's at least have the honesty of knowing that my face and body are what you like. The person inside was never important to you. I doubt whether you know the smallest thing about that person . . . whether or not she cared for someone else when you married her. You never once thought to ask, did you, Paul? It just didn't matter so long as you got what you wanted."

The car swept round another bend, and the glittering lights of the harbour were suddenly much closer to them. A yacht rode at anchor about half a mile out and snatches of music and laughter floated across the water.

"Did you care for somebody else?" Paul asked quietly.

Domini studied his profile, moulded with all the perfection of Grecian art, and cold and hard as the marble the Greeks had worked in. How she longed to say outright that she *did* care for another man. That she had never stopped caring; that he had all the tenderness she would never give to any other man.

But even in her frustration and anger, fear of Paul had the upper hand and she turned aside to say with forced coolness: "What would it have mattered to you? You would not have shown any compassion for my feelings . . . you're made of stone where I'm concerned."

"Not quite," he drawled. "A man of stone would not be moved by a face or a body. Nor hurt a little by their coldness."

She shivered as though at his touch, and drew her wrap closer about her. What had Paul expected? Not affection, surely, from a woman who had given herself to him to save her family from the scandal sheets and the pointing finger of scorn?

No, he could never have expected affection, but there had been a night in Athens when she had recognised that in some ways Paul was curiously isolated from people, and lonely. He was thirty-six, but he sometimes seemed a man who had stepped into the twilight of a much older man.

Recollection of that night returned clearly to Domini. All day they had been at the races, where he had gradually developed a severe headache. Moved by his obvious pain, she had urged him to return to the hotel, where they had dined upstairs on the cool of their balcony, not talking much, but with something between them that came close to companionship. When he had gone to his room, and she had lain alone in hers, she had heard him pacing up and down for more than an hour.

Up and down, like a caged tiger, while she turned restlessly in her bed and wondered if conscience could be troubling him. The smoke of a chain of cheroots had drifted under the adjoining door, and once or twice she had lifted herself on one elbow, close to a compulsion to go in to him. Her hand had been on the bedcovers, about to throw them back, when his pacing had stopped and she heard him get into bed.

She had known from the deep-etched lines in his face the following morning that he had hardly closed his eyes. With harshness, almost, he had pulled her into his arms in her silk robe and crushed to nothing the polite enquiry on her lips. "So you heard me pacing about?" He had laughed without humour. "It was that, or this, Domini." And again his mouth had taken forcibly what she would not give willingly . . .

Now, as the car swung into the drive of the Venetian Mask and ground to a halt on the gravel, Paul turned to face her, an elbow resting on the wheel. His eyes

112

dwelt on her lips, as though he had in mind those kisses she forced him to take.

"You may have Kara to stay with us if you would like that," he said. "But it will distress the child if she learns it is bitter honey that we share."

"Have I not played my part reasonably well up to now?" Domini's pulses gave a jolt at the way he had put it. "I should like Kara to stay with us not entirely for my own sake, but because I feel she isn't all that happy at the house of your aunt. You must have sensed this yourself, Paul?"

He inclined his head. "Since her widowhood, my aunt has grown very possessive of Nikos, and it might be better for Kara to come to us. Always before I have been away from the island a great deal and my house would have been too lonely for her. Now things are different. Now I have a wife—yes, by all means invite Kara to stay."

"She loves you, Paul," Domini said quietly. "I shall do nothing to destroy that. I'm not—vindictive."

"Ah, no," he touched her hair and his mouth was almost gentle for a moment. "No, you are sensitive in the extreme, and you find me hard to understand. Perhaps in time you will understand."

The flashing and dimming lights of the Venetian Mask played over her face as they sat there in the car . . . Domini's heart pounded, half with apprehension, half with secret longing that Barry would be here tonight and they would dance together.

She stepped from the car, heard behind her the decisive slam of the door and the crunch of gravel as Paul caught up with her and took her elbow in a light grip as they mounted the steps of the club. An attendant at the door greeted Paul as a member, and inside the entrance a girl handed him a black mask, and Domini a gold one. She gave an excited little laugh as she put hers on. "I feel like a sixteenth-century coquette in this," she smiled.

She saw the tiger gleam of Paul's eyes through the slits of his mask and thought he looked satanic with the black line of his brows above it, and his teeth showing in a quick smile. "Come along, Domini," he said, and he led her into the large, romantically lit Venetian room where couples were whirling to a waltz, or sitting in alcoves on lunette couches talking together and looking mysterious in their masks.

The walls were painted with murals of dusky gold palaces and green canals; the soaring Bridge of Sighs and gondolas gliding like dark swans beneath it.

Domini gazed around her, her lips half parted, the breath catching in her throat as she saw someone tall shouldering his way through the dancers. His mask was crimson, and she would have known him anywhere, in any throng, because of his leonine head.

He greeted them, and then said to Paul: "May I dance with your wife, Mr. Stephanos?"

"By all means," Paul said coolly, and he stood back in the shadows of a columned alcove as Barry swept Domini in among the waltzing couples.

She told herself it was the smoke that made her eyes misty as the years between fell away and she moved to music in Barry's arms once again.

For minutes on end they danced without speaking, circling the floor as though they were up in the clouds. "Domini," he spoke her name huskily, "my heart nearly stopped when you appeared on that terrace this afternoon. Kara told me that her brother had married a girl named Domini, but I couldn't believe, didn't want to believe that it was *you*. Not *my* Domini."

Tears blurred her eyes when he said that, and she stumbled and was caught close against him. That frightened her, for Paul was now in conversation with Alexis and there was a long mirror at the back of the bar that reflected the dance floor and the circling couples. She pulled hastily away from contact with Barry. "We must be careful," she whispered, and joy at being with him had sharpened to fear.

"But I've got to talk to you—alone." His fingers bit into her waist. His eyes blazed down into hers through his mask, and his mouth looked dangerous. She wanted to put her hand against his lips, to press into silence the words that wouldn't be silenced.

"I love you, Domini," he said, speaking deep in his throat. "I've never stopped."

"I'm married, Barry," she replied. "And this—this talk of love has got to stop."

"I want to shout it from the roof," he said dangerously. "And I shall if you don't come out into the garden with me—and tell me why you married a man you don't love."

"H-How can you know that?" she gasped, beginning to feel dizzy from dancing, and from being still too close for comfort to a man other than Paul. Her eyes sought her husband over Barry's shoulder. He and Alexis were now seated on stools, and he seemed for the moment content to be entertained by her. Her masked eyes, Domini noticed, were fixed on his face.

"Let's slip away, now, and talk," Barry urged. "While your husband is engrossed in the seductive Alexis."

"I-I shouldn't—" she was afraid, and yet she needed so much to talk alone with him. But it was hardly possible, here at the Venetian Mask . . .

The dance music ceased and as the cabaret was announced couples moved back off the floor to tables and alcoves. The lights dimmed once more, the music began softly, beckoning out from between curtains a slim dancer in filmy trousers and a glittering halter. She came with deliberation into the centre of the floor, where she hovered in a ruby spotlight like a dragonfly in a flame.

Domini stood in the shadows beside Barry, her heart beating fast at his closeness as the dancer lifted dark-skinned hands above her head and clicked her finger castanets. The music quickened, she began to dance, possessed of all the sinuous grace and hypnotic attraction of a snake-goddess. The click-click of her castanets sounded like seashells knocking together in a pagan grotto; the curtains of time parted as she whirled and leapt and arched backwards until her long black hair swept the floor. There might well have been Venetian galleys in the harbour and armoured captains in the audience. Telethusa danced again in that picturesque room, and with every eye following her every movement it was almost too easy for two people in the shadows to move backwards out of glass doors open to the garden, the man urging the woman with hands that would not be denied.

"Come over here among the trees." Barry pulled Domini into their shade and fragrance. " 'The gods see everywhere'," he quoted laughingly.

"Don't!" She gave a shiver, both from his words and his touch as he held her against a tangle of honeysuckle. "I-I must go in when the music stops," she said uneasily.

"Afraid of your husband?" His voice grew angry, and jealous.

"No—it isn't that."

"What is it, then, his satanic brand of charm? Was it that you couldn't resist?" He took her by the shoulders and held them bruisingly. "I've got to know why you married Paul Stephanos. Why, Domini, when it was understood between us—without words—that one day we would marry?"

116

"One day, Barry?" Her smile was wrenched. "You went away and you never wrote. I thought you had forgotten me."

"That isn't true." The arrogance of knowledge rang in his voice. "We pledged ourselves to each other the evening before I went away, and you knew I meant it when I said I would come back to you. You were so young, Domini, so carefree in your freedom, and there was so much I wanted to do with my freedom before we married. I wanted to put on canvas what men like Rodin have created out of stone, and I needed the utter absorption of being alone while I worked at what I wanted to do."

"And have you succeeded, Barry?" She gazed up at his face in a shaft of starlight, and her fingers crushed the honeysuckle against which he held her . . . within kissing distance.

"I've been to many places," he said, his fingertips against her cheeks, "and here in Greece I found the light so exulting that I couldn't stop painting. Mount Ida and the cave of Zeus like a leering eye. Dark Naxian fishermen. The beautiful, frightening battlements of Rhodes. The Greeks believe that men are clay fired in flame; they have faced up to the darkness in the soul, and this was what I wanted for my work, and for us, Domini. For *us*."

The silence between them was somehow intensified by the music of Telethusa, its rhythm ebbed and flowed like pain and passion.

"It has always been a pastime of Greeks to trap birds in a net." Barry touched a hand to her hair. "And they've always had a taste for wild honey."

"Is that your definition of my marriage?" A pulse was beating quickly in her throat.

"You aren't happy with the man. I know! I've seen

your eyes and how they glow blue as anchusas when you're happy."

"Happiness isn't the whole of living, Barry."

"Nor is drinking wine, or singing songs, or making love." He tilted her chin, and added harshly: "Tears and kisses have made you lovelier than I remember you —what is between you and that brooding Greek, love or hate?"

"I can only answer that he stands between you and me, Barry. I belong to him. He's my husband."

"And have you known a happy moment with him since he became your husband?" His voice grated.

"Yes—ah, you look shocked, Barry, as though it wasn't possible." She gave a bitter-sweet laugh. "He isn't a monster. Paul has the power to make a woman feel—almost a goddess in his arms."

"Was it for the lovemaking that you married him?" Barry's fingers were bruising her arms. "The kisses of Apollo?"

Her eyes closed from the pain of his grip, and from the inward pain of knowing that she could never tell him the truth about her marriage. Love of family was fool's gold, he had said long ago. Something you surely dug out of your heart at your own expense. He had been able to say it because he had no family and had been reared in a home for orphans. Uncle Martin and Douglas had been her family from babyhood.

"We must go in," she said, grown wary again, on her guard for footfalls and the tall, dark figure of her husband. "The music has stopped and people are clapping."

She attempted to pull away from him, but he held her forcibly within inches of his lips. "Kiss me first, Domini," he said. "It's a forfeit I'm entitled to, in the circumstances."

"No, Barry—" her heart was in her throat, for each rustle, each shadow, each second she stayed out here with him was increasing her nervousness. "You'll be at the party tomorrow night. We shall see each other then, and dance together."

"Domini, you little fool," his low, laughing breath fanned her face. "You and I can never be friends . . . we were meant to be closer than that to each other."

"What was meant has no meaning now," she said desperately. "Neither of us can be compared any more to those youthful innocents who did their courting on the keel of an upturned boat on the sands at Knightley. The girl with the pony-tail and the carefree eyes doesn't exist any more—can't you see that? Domini Stephanos has taken her place."

"No, the sweet familiar is still there," he insisted, "and added to it the enchanting unknown. Be grown up, Domini. If you think—"

"And if you think I can live in a dream world and pretend Paul doesn't exist, then you're very much mistaken, Barry." She met his eyes, hers stormy. "He's a Greek and he's very possessive, and nothing can alter the fact that I married him."

"You're *his* possession, eh?" Barry spoke harshly. "If you knew what it does to me—to imagine you in his arms!"

"I belong in his arms." It was a cold statement of fact.

"Yes, he has the claims," Barry tilted her chin and studied her pale, gold-masked face, "but I have something else."

"Have you?" she said shakily.

"I have your heart, Domini . . . I'm sure of it."

Everything was hushed and still when he said that, it was as though the vines and tamarisks stopped moving to listen. A dangerously sweet moment, fraught with memories of youthful promises, and freedom. Domini felt the touch of the familiar hands. Tears ached in her throat, and she was swept by a stormy longing to reveal everything to Barry. "Take me away," she wanted to say to him. "There are caiques in the harbour for hire, and we could be miles away by morning. Take me away, Barry, and we'll be young and carefree as we once were . . ."

"Why did you marry him, Domini?" Barry's voice matched the urgency of his hands. "I know he's as handsome as the devil, that he has position and power, but none of those would matter a jot to you . . . unless you loved him. Domini, *tell me!*"

"I-I can't tell you—the reason involves another person—"

"A man?"

"Yes."

"Ye gods! What happened to you, Domini? What changed the lovely, gay-hearted kid I fell in love with?"

She shook her head, wordless, and feeling the slackening of his grip she broke free of him and hastened back into the Venetian Mask. Fig-boughs caught at her hair as she brushed past them, and she didn't know that a crushed honeysuckle was clinging to the lace of her dress.

People were dancing again, and her eyes swept the couples. One couple made all the others look mediocre —Paul with a smiling Alexis in his arms. Then a hand touched Domini's arm and she turned to meet Kara's eyes. They scanned her face and her hair, then almost casually Kara brushed the honeysuckle from Domini's dress. "Nikki has deserted me to dance with blonde and gigly Susie Vanhusen," she smiled. "Paul is dancing with Alexis, but you must not mind."

"I don't mind," said Domini, and she saw a frown wrinkle Kara's mask, and the flash of her eyes towards the glass doors that now framed the tall figure of Barry Sothern, with his lion-mane of hair.

He looked directly across at Domini and Kara, and though both he and Domini were masked, she had the uneasy feeling that the girl beside her had unmasked them. The toe of Kara's green slipper crushed the honeysuckle petals . . . she knew that her brother's wife and Barry had been talking together in the garden . . . but not as the strangers they pretended to be.

CHAPTER TEN

"KALI MERA!" Kara came to join Domini on her balcony for breakfast. Domini had overslept after their late return from the Venetian Mask, finding Paul gone from their bed when she awoke. Kara, busily helping herself to grilled roes and tomatoes, informed her that he and Nikos had gone to the Turkish baths down in town.

"Nikos is a real charmer," Domini said as she poured coffee and added cream. The morning was a golden one, and the sun stroked her hair, loose on the shoulders of her wrapper.

"He is a handsome mother's boy." Kara wrinkled her nose as she tucked into her breakfast. "Aunt Sophula need not worry that I am after her precious son. I like him for a cousin, but he has only to pull my hair and she finds holes to pick in me. I am fed up with it."

"Poor little Kara!" Domini smiled over the rim of her coffee cup. "How would you like to come and stay with Paul and me at the house on the eagle's crag?"

Kara stopped eating and stared at Domini with dark eager eyes "I would like it more than anything," she said. "But are you serious? You and Paul are so newly married—would I not be in the way?"

"It's a big house," Domini laughed. "There is ample room for a whippet like you."

"What does Paul say? You have asked his permission?"

"Yes, I have asked the master's permission," Domini said dryly. "He agrees with me that you are restless here at your aunt's house. He wants you as much as I do"

"Domini, I am gratified." Kara's eyes shone like dewberries. "I have longed to be more with Paul, but I don't want to be in the way."

"How could you be in the way when we are both fond of you?" Domini buttered a slice of toast and piled rich Greek honey on to it.

"A honeymoon is for two people," Kara said simply. "It is an interlude of great delicacy and I don't wish to —to strike a false note."

"My dear," Domini gave a gentle laugh, "no one with your sensitive ear could ever strike a false note. Both Paul and I feel that you'll be happier with us, and I shall appreciate and enjoy your company while Paul is busy at work in his office each day."

"It will be fun." The sparkle came back into Kara's eyes. "There is the beach below the house, the caves to explore, and the dolphins that play and swim in the lagoon. Paul will not be working all of the time, will he? He loves to swim . . . he and Loukas could always swim like sea-cats."

Kara pushed her plate to one side and took a peach from a nest of leaves. Her lashes threw shadows on her cheeks as she ran her fingers over the velvety fruit. "Loukas liked to go deep diving, you know." Her voice shook and she had to wait a moment to compose it. "There is a world of colour and mystery below the surface of the sea, and often he would go down with a camera fitted to take undersea photographs, wearing an air-mask and looking like a shiny merman. He would take photographs of the tentacled anemones, the trees of coral, the grottoes that might have been carved for Undine. Loukas was clever at his hobby, and like all hobbies it could absorb him beyond time, fear, anything."

Paul's sister glanced up, and found Domini regarding

her with eyes whose depth and compassion was intensified by her dark double lashes.

"We were out in Paul's boat," Kara went on, "and Loukas went over the side with his photographic equipment almost as soon as we had headed out into the Ionian. Alexis was sun-basking on the deck. Paul was at the helm, and I was playing my zither and we were making up comical verses and singing them. It was a day like now, Domini, with the Grecian isles all hazy and green, and the sea-mews flying down to meet their reflections in the water. There was such a feeling of peace . . . until Alexis remarked in her lazy, not really concerned way, that Loukas must be seducing Undine on the sea-bed, he had been down so long."

Kara's nails dug into the peach and juice ran out. "Alexis is fond of making such remarks and we had grown used to them, but Paul did not laugh. He called our *mikro* up from the galley to take the helm; he added that he was going down to see if Loukas was all right, and he changed into diving gear . . ."

The girl's English had been faltering for minutes; now her story was interspersed with Greek words and Domini was leaning forward on one elbow, listening intently.

"Paul went a long way down," Kara said. "Searching, searching for Loukas. There is a point of depth where you can remain only a few minutes before you risk your supply of air . . . and it was then that Paul found Loukas. He brought him to the surface, quickly, and we pulled them into the boat . . . Paul knelt to strip off his brother's aqualung harness, then all at once he crumpled over himself and he looked terrible, his eyes rolled back in his head, and Alexis screamed out that they were both dead."

Kara gave a shudder. "What had happened was that he had surfaced too rapidly on a low supply of air,

124

which is very dangerous and can cause death or paralysis. Alexis got calm again and gave Paul artificial respiration, and though he was breathing normally again by the time we put into harbour, he did not regain consciousness until later in hospital. At the insistence of the doctors he remained there for some days, in case a complication should develop. Loukas . . . he was dead. Paul had found him below an undersea cliff of coral, the jagged kind that had formed into rocks . . ."

"Don't talk about it any more, Kara." Domini's own hand was none too steady as she pressed the girl's thin fingers. "I am sure Loukas couldn't have suffered."

"Paul said the same when I visited him in hospital." Kara gave Domini a shaky smile. "It was for Paul that I told you about Loukas. He has not always had happiness in his life, and I was so glad for him when he wrote to tell me he had taken an English girl for his wife. We feel close to the English because it has been a custom since Grandfather's time for us to be taught your language. Because of the shipping line, you understand, and doing so much business with English-speaking people."

"You speak English perfectly," Domini smiled. "My Greek will never be as good—look, how about taking me on an exploration of the harbour when we've had breakfast? Perhaps Nikos could be persuaded to come with us. Paul, the work fiend, has brought some correspondence with him which he proposes to answer, and I'm dying to see more of Andelos."

"What a good idea!" Kara brightened up and took a big juicy bite out of her peach. "Today is Sunday, so Nikki is free from his work at the local office. Nikki is. very ambitious, you know."

"I would say that ambition runs in the blood of your menfolk, Kara." Domini wore a thoughtful smile as she gazed out to sea, following the vermilion-sailed boat that was etched with its shadow against the blue water. The tangy scent of the sea was in her nostrils, Kara's story in her mind. She had never doubted Paul's courage, or the love of family that ran strongly in his Greek blood. She knew how generous he could be, and she could give him respect, even sometimes the shaken response of the moment, but there was no sense of security in her relationship.

Only the loved had security; people grew tired of their caprices, the things they took for their passing pleasure.

Kara dashed away to get ready for their walk, and Domini was in her bedroom, fastening a necklace of white beads, when Paul came in. He looked overpoweringly big and clean, his hair a cropped riot of curls from the steam-bath, his eyes, as they met Domini's in the mirror, a sheer amber between the density of his lashes. Handsome as the devil, Barry had said, and she tensed as his hands closed over her shoulders and he bent to kiss the side of her neck.

"You smell like mimosa," he said, lifting her from the dressing-stool and turning her to face him. She wore a sleeveless white dress appliquéd with mimosa sprays on the hip, and tiny hidden nerves rippled as Paul's eyes travelled over her. She did not resist as he drew her close against him. Her fingertips pressed into his shoulders, then slid nerveless down the steel-like ridges of his muscles as her lips were lost under his in a long possessive kiss.

She breathed the familiar spicy tang of his after-shave, and lay quiescent under his kiss. Then quite suddenly his hands bit into her sides. "You little piece of ice," he muttered, "kiss me for once!" And gentleness was gone as he tipped her over his arm and forced her lips to soften and yield to his.

When he finally lifted his head and allowed her to stand upright, the world for Domini was spinning and she had to clutch at the dressing-table. Paul's teeth glinted in a narrow smile. "Domini, *mia,* don't look like that," he mocked. "You might strike me dead with such a look."

"It would take more than a look from me to kill you, Paul," she said, still shaken and angry at the way he had forced a response from her to that savage kiss. Her lips still hurt, and she knew she would find bruises on her waist from his grip.

He shook his curly black head in mock reproof. "As I have told you before, my dear, I am not so invulnerable. I have my Achilles heel like other men, and you might even miss me a little—who knows?—if the keeper of the door were to suddenly open it and call me through it."

She looked him over when he said that, and the dark, pagan head that was carried so arrogantly on the brown column of a neck. "What am I to you?" she felt compelled to ask.

He considered her question, his fingers playing idly with her necklace. "Perhaps the fabric of dreams," he murmured. "The pearl I trapped in my ear—as our artist friend put it."

"The successful man's status symbol," she corrected coldly. "Strange, but I should never have thought that you would be content with less than adoration, Paul, the complete sublimation of a woman's heart."

"Circumstances sometimes decree what we must be contented with," he replied, with irony. "What do you want, Domini, a dream knight?"

"That would be pleasant," she rejoined, thinking of Barry the boy who on an upturned boat with the sunset in his hair had seemed like one.

"Galahads on white chargers exist only in the land of

127

fable," he said dryly. "You will have to content yourself with a Lancelot."

"Lancelot the black knight," she quipped. "But he won the heart of the queen, didn't he?"

Paul tilted Domini's chin and his eyes held hers, made devilish by the scar above the right one. "What if I asked for your heart, Domini?" he said.

"That broken thing?" She forced a laugh. "It was something you didn't want when it was intact . . . don't you remember what you said to me on our wedding day? That you had no time to spend on the triviality of being loved."

"The word I used was 'liked,' " he corrected.

"Was it?" She shrugged. "Surely a man can't expect to be loved if he isn't liked?"

"There are many proofs that love has little to do with the lesser emotions." He feathered her chin with his thumb and added abruptly: "What are your plans for the morning?"

"Kara's going to take me on an exploration of the harbour. We're hoping that Nikos will go with us."

"Good, be a child for a day with those two." Suddenly his hands were cradling her face and a quick smile warmed his eyes. "Forget your tyrant of a husband."

She gazed up at him, at the tyrant who could be gentle at times. Her heart seemed to draw a sigh as on impulse she went on tiptoe and brushed a kiss across his cheek. He made no comment, but turned from her and took up her raffia handbag and pushed some notes into it. "You are bound to see things you will want to buy," he said casually. "Andelos, like London, has its Petticoat Lane."

They drove down to the harbour in Nikos's low-slung car, where he parked in a patch of shade. The trio then

128

walked under an old gateway through which a flock of sheep bleated and tumbled, and entered the alleyways and arcades of the market-place.

The air was rich with spicy smells, and people clustered round the many stalls and haggled in loud good-natured voices. Squid hung from hooks, and there were panniers and pyramids of exotic-looking vegetables and fruits. Cradles, quilts, pitchers and pewter were among the many articles for sale, and outside a bakery Domini paused to admire the coils and lengths of fresh-baked bread. "I can't resist the smell of hot bread and sesame seeds," she said. They bought *brioches* and ate the sugary things walking along.

Those few carefree hours down at the harbour passed happily. With Paul's *drachmas* in her purse, Domini couldn't resist treating her companions and herself to odd, delightful little presents. Then all at once Kara caught at Domini's arm and pointed to a gipsy sitting on the harbour wall with a basket beside him. He looked like an old brigand, with baggy trousers tucked into knee-boots and wearing a grubby coloured shirt. There was a knotted kerchief about his head, and he had black moustachios with a boot-polish lustre to them.

When the three young people paused some steps away from him, he dug a hand into his basket and brought it out with charms cupped in his large brown palm. He said something in Greek, and Nikos informed Domini that they were being invited to choose and buy a charm. He would tell their fortunes from the charms they chose.

Kara couldn't resist the idea and she ran forward to take a look at the charms. She chose an anchor of brass and crossed the old man's palm with silver. She was anxious about something, he told her. She wished for stability and felt herself to be adrift; also the sea was in her blood, and one day she would cross it with a tall dark man who was not a stranger.

"Can he mean Paul?" Kara said wonderingly, and Domini smiled a little at her innocence.

"Now it is your turn, *kyria*." Nikos gave Domini a cheeky smile. "Find out what fate is in store for you."

"No—" she stepped back reluctantly as the gipsy thrust out his charm-filled palm, his eyes fixed upon her face.

"Come, it is only a game," Nikos laughed. "A beautiful girl need not fear that fate is going to be unkind."

Domini's heart was beating very fast. She knew it was silly of her not to want to join in the game, but the gipsy had said some curiously perceptive things about Kara. The girl was troubled by a sense of insecurity at the present time, and her feeling for Nikki went deeper than she suspected . . . Nikos, the tall dark man who was not a stranger.

"Be a sport and take a charm, Domini," Kara coaxed.

And almost blindly Domini delved into the outstretched palm and took the first charm that her fingers touched . . . a tiny female figure with long brass hair binding her body. Domini crossed the gipsy's palm with silver and felt the jetty scrutiny of his eyes. He spoke to her in Greek, but she couldn't understand him, and Nikos translated what he said to her.

"Why," Nikos gave a laugh of frustration, "the old rogue says, *kyria*, that you know already what the charm signifies and he need not tell you. Do you know?"

Domini was glad that the wide brim of her raffia hat shielded her eyes, for it had shaken her that she had chosen so significant a charm from the gipsy. *She was bound and could not escape,* and her fingers clenched over the charm as she said: "Come on, you two," and ran down some nearby steps to the seashore. There were several caiques drawn up on the sands and their shadows had hidden her before Kara, lingering with Nikos beside the gipsy, realised the direction she had taken. They turned back into the market-place thinking she had gone that way, and it was several minutes before Domini glanced over her shoulder and saw that she was walking alone on the seashore.

She stood hesitant there at the water's edge, the sea breeze blowing against her face and neck. How cool and tangy those breezes, and how peaceful to be utterly alone for a few minutes. She was reluctant to turn back towards the noisy market area, and spotting a bollard she made for it and rested there. She knew where Nikos' car was parked and she told herself she would make for it as soon as the sea air had driven away the slight ache at her temples.

Domini drew off her raffia hat and let the breeze blow through her hair. There were only a few bare-footed fishermen mending nets on the shore, and a woman with hoisted black skirts was hunting for shellfish. It was a tranquil scene, with the varying blues of the sea as a background, and the distant mountains above the Balkans.

Too tranquil these moments to last, and a chill feathered along Domini's neck and arms as a cloud rolled over the sun and the shore turned dull and grey. She picked up her raffia bag and rose from the bollard. She turned to go in search of Kara and Nikos . . . then backed away with a small startled cry as she found herself face to face with the person she had least expected to see this morning—Barry Sothern.

They stood looking at each other, the rising wind ruffling the blond hair above Barry's slow-smiling eyes. Eyes that appraised the coming and going colour in Domini's cheeks. "I saw your honey hair blowing in the breeze, but I came warily in case my wishful thinking had made a Greek fishergirl look for all the world like Domini Dane."

"Domini Stephanos," she reminded him.

He shook his blond head and tossed the stub of his cigarette into a rockpool. "I know the girl I saw as I came down on the shore." He raised his eyes and took in the darkening sky. "We're in for a downpour from the look of those clouds. Look, Domini, my cottage isn't far from here—how about coming back for a drink?"

"I don't think I ought to, Barry. Kara and Nikos will be waiting for me at the car—I came with them to have a look round the market and we got separated."

"Will it matter if you stay separated another half hour?" He smiled down at her coaxingly. "Domini, you were always a little too dutiful. Do you remember how you used to worry about creeping out of school to meet me?"

"I—don't want to talk about the old days." Her fingernails bit through the raffia rim of the hat she was holding. "It's been nice seeing you again, Barry—"

"Here," he closed a restraining hand about her arm, "you aren't running away from me like that."

"I must, Barry." She gazed up at him pleadingly, "Be a good boy and let me go."

He broke into a grin that made him look as sardonic as Pan, the god of mischief. "I'm inviting you to my cottage for a drink, not to a *pied-à-terre* for some clandestine lovemaking—anyway, you don't have to tell anyone that you came with me."

"Someone might see us," she hedged.

"You could always say that you came to look at my paintings." His eyes were mocking her, and then he gave a gasping laugh and swept an arm around her as the clouds broke and the rain came pelting down.

"Come on, run," he said, and there was no escaping him as he ran her across the sands, up some winding steps, and across rows of shiny wet cobbles to a lane where a whitewashed cottage was tucked away. She stood under the porch with her white dress clinging to her as he opened the door and hustled her along a passage and into his sitting room. She took off her hat and gave it a shake, looking round her and smiling at the bachelor untidiness of the room. A divan heaped with Greek cushions, breakfast things still on the table, canvases stacked against a wall, a profusion of pot plants on the wide sill of the small-paned window.

"My studio is upstairs," Barry said, taking her raffia bag and her hat. "Your dress is wet, you ought to take it off and let it dry."

She looked at him swiftly. "I'll get you a dressing-robe," he added mischievously.

Domini felt her dress and found it pretty damp. "All right," she said, without looking at him.

He went out of the room and a minute later tossed in to her a bold Paisley dressing-robe. "I'll make coffee while you're disrobing, Domini," she heard the smile in his voice. "Do you like Turkish coffee?"

"Yes, please." She could smell English cigarette smoke on his robe, and as she tied the waist-cord and felt the silk against her bare arms and shoulders, she gave a little shiver of stolen pleasure at being here in Barry's cottage . . . where, as lightning clashed like crossed rapiers in the sky, it looked as though she was going to be marooned for an hour or more. During that time Kara and Nikos would be bound to give up their search for her and return home . . . she didn't dare to think what Paul would assume.

She arranged her dress over the back of a chair to dry, then carried Barry's breakfast tray out to the kitchen. "Haven't you a housekeeper?" she asked.

"I need the freedom of living in a muddle," he said lazily. He was at the stove brewing their coffee, and his wet hair looked as though it had been combed with his fingers. The tousled look made him very endearing, and the years fell away as Domini gazed at him in his paint-splashed cords and striped T-shirt.

"You should always wear a masculine robe that's miles too big for you." He took her in from head to toe. "You look cuddly and rather helpless."

Domini scraped eggshells into the bin under the sink and when she straightened up her cheeks were faintly pink. "I hope you're going to show me some of your Greek paintings now I'm here," she said.

"Warning me to behave myself?" He came over and stood looking down at her as she started to wash up his breakfast things. "What are we going to do about us, Domini?" he murmured.

"Look at your paintings and drink Turkish coffee." She scraped busily at a blob of yolk on the side of an eggcup.

"And pretend we're mere acquaintances?" He insinuated a hand up the wide sleeve of his robe. "It won't work, darling. We belong together, you and I. Circumstances tried to part us, but we met again on this faraway Greek island, a sure indication that it isn't just a legend that an unbreakable cord of love binds some people together from birth. Inevitably, over the years, it tightens to draw them together and nothing, not time, distance, or anyone can keep them from finding unity."

She glanced up at him, her every instinct in accord with what he said. Love didn't just happen. A mystic force did work to draw two people together, so closely that nothing, not even death could ever part them again.

"What about Paul?" she asked quietly. "You seem to be forgetting him."

"There is a way of forgetting him." Barry took her by the shoulders and his eyes were a dark serious brown as he gazed down at her. "Domini, we could go away together."

134

CHAPTER ELEVEN

"DO you hear me, Domini?" Barry's hands tightened on her shoulders. "We'll run away together, and Stephanos will quietly divorce you——"

"He wouldn't." Domini shook her head, knowing too well the ruthless side to Paul. "He would never make it possible for us to be happy together, Barry."

"Would you find it so hard to be happy without the legalities, honey?" Barry started to draw her against him, but she pressed her hands to his chest and held off from his embrace.

"If you snatch at what you want, Barry, it doesn't bring happiness," she said with conviction. "I've already tasted the bitterness of that . . . I know all about the distrust that can haunt two people who aren't sure of each other. We would never know the security and peace of a true marriage. Never feel sure of each other, knowing that I belong in every legal sense to another man."

"You don't love him, Domini." Barry's eyes were storm-dark under his fair, tousled hair. "I know full well he forced you to marry him—he's that sort. This island abounds with tales about the Stephanos clan and how ruthlessly they fought in the rebellion. The islanders still boast about Paul's fierceness as a sixteen-year-old *andarte* and how he crawled yards, still tossing grenades after having taken one almost in his face. From all accounts he should have died from that wound. There's more than a hint of superstition attached to the fact that he recovered from something that would have killed a normal man."

Domini thought of the jagged scar that marred Paul's temple, and the headaches from which he still suffered after all these years, and she felt an urge to defend him. He was Greek to his bones, he loved fiercely the land for which he would have died, a mere boy.

"The coffee's bubbling over," she said.

"Darn the coffee—!"

"Please," she broke free of Barry, crossed the room and took the pot off the stove. "You carry in the cups and we'll have our coffee in your sitting-room," she added.

They shared a long silence as they sat in the other room, listening to the rain and watching the lightning dispel the shadows for fleeting seconds. "I should never have done it, should I, Domini," Barry spoke raggedly, "left you in England when I loved you—when I knew you loved me. God, what makes us do the things we do, the misguided, driven things that mess up our lives?"

"You were ambitious, and we were both very young." Domini met the regret of Barry's eyes. "Did we really believe that we would meet again, or did we share a dream that we didn't really wish to put to the test of reality?"

"Believing that, Domini, won't absolve us from the regret we're now feeling," he said moodily. "I was a fool, the biggest. You were always too lovely to have escaped the eye of other men, but I went away as though I left you an enchanted schoolgirl sitting on the keel of a boat with your honey hair blowing in the sea breezes there to stay until I returned to kiss you awake. It drags out my heart that it was Paul Stephanos who did that." Barry stared at her. "How did you meet? You haven't told me."

Domini explained that her cousin had worked in a shipping-line office of Paul's, and that their eventual meeting had been inevitable.

"Was there a family reason for your marriage?" The question jumped at her, and she flinched as though at a

136

flash of lightning. "What a Victorian question, Barry!" She gave a laugh that cost her a lot. "Girls these days aren't coerced into marriage by their families."

"You admitted last night that someone else was involved." He leaned forward on the hassock on which he was sitting. "You said it was a man—*was it Douglas*?"

Her heart took a leap into her throat. Barry had grown shrewd. The boy on the beach was lost in the man who had become a painter of some renown. Suddenly she was afraid of him, aware of being far more vulnerable as the disillusioned wife of another man than she had been as a romantic girl of seventeen.

And as though he read her mind, he said: "You look about seventeen at the moment, lost in my robe with your hair all tousled. Wouldn't do," a wicked glint came into his eyes, "for that husband of yours to walk in on us right now. He'd break my neck, eh?"

Instinctively her gaze went to the door, and she heard Barry laugh in his throat, then felt his hand take hold of her left one. When she looked at him he was examining the wide gold band that was the symbol of Paul's ownership, and the sapphire, enclosed in twin swirls of diamonds afire with all that passion that Paul had a legal right to feel.

His fingers tightened and the ring seemed to bite her to the bone. Their eyes locked, then he was kneeling by her chair and holding her, and after the first struggling moment she couldn't deny herself the comfort of pressing her face to his shoulder and breathing the smoke of English cigarettes that clung to him. She closed her eyes and pretended she was seventeen again and that the sound of the rain was the sound of the sea, lapping the beach at Knightley.

"We'll find a way to be together," Barry murmured. "You shan't stay with Stephanos against your will."

Domini heard him, and yet she wasn't really listening, for over his shoulder her gaze had been caught by a canvas hanging against the whitewashed wall. It was a beach after being racked by storm, the water seemed to heave in the aftermath of distress and there were rocks like the broken remnants of a fallen castle. Seaweed was strewn across the sands, taking the shape of arms with all emotion wrung out of them. A strange blue light shifted over the scene, and a tiny ray led the eye upwards, through the clouds to where a patch of brightness gleamed in the sky.

Art in all its forms, Domini knew, was a representation of all human conflict, and she felt that impact of Barry's painting right through her being. Saw in it her own clamour of the heart, her yearning for the happiness that might be clutched at, won back, coaxed into more than a fitful ray.

"When did you paint that beach scene, Barry?" she asked. "That one over there, on the wall by the window."

He sat back on his heels and glanced over his shoulder at the painting. "I got the idea soon after we parted at Knightley. It's funny," his eyes came back to her face, "I've had several big offers for it, but I can't sell it. In some ways it's cruder than what I'm doing now, but it has something—depth, a sort of agony."

"It has," she said quietly, "what has to be faced between us, Barry—your painting takes first place in your life. It did when we met, and over the years we were apart. It does now, and in your heart you know it."

"Yes, I know my painting's important to me," he admitted. "But so are you, Domini. I want you."

She gave a little shiver, for Paul had said the same thing. *I want you.* She looked at Barry and she had to put to the test the love he had talked about. "Can't we just be friends?" she asked.

He knelt on the Greek rug looking up at her, at the pale honey smoothness of her skin, the blue eyes set with a jewel-like precision under the fine eyebrows that were several shades darker than her honey-coloured hair. His glance dropped to her mouth with its sensitive upper lip and tempestuous lower one. His own mouth twisted savagely. "You're asking a lot, aren't you, Domini?" he said. "You're not the kind of a girl a man wants just for a friend—hasn't living with Paul Stephanos taught you what men want of you?"

She had invited the truth, but still it hurt that he should say it outright. She got to her feet and went over to the window. The rain had long since lost its fury and the sky had cleared a little. The thunder had died away.

"I'd better be making a move," she said. "Paul will come looking for me otherwise."

Barry came behind her and swung her to face him. A nerve was kicking in his jaw. "What do you want, Domini, a boy-girl relationship such as we had at Knightley? Well, it just isn't possible. You must either go away with me on my terms, or stay with Stephanos on his."

"I know." She spoke quietly. "I can't dictate the terms because I don't mean enough to either of you."

"Domini!"

"It's true, Barry." Her eyes were steady on his face. "I'd like to change into my dress now, and comb my hair. May I use your bedroom?"

"Of course." He went over to the door and held it open, and as she passed him with her dress over her arm, she felt him looking at her with angry bewilderment. He directed her up a narrow winding stairway to his room, and she went in, closed the door behind her and proceeded to tidy herself up.

She felt curiously empty of emotion as she combed her hair in front of a mirror on the chest of drawers. There were studs and a pair of hairbrushes lying here, also a box of sugared almonds and a piece of amethyst crystal he had probably picked up on the beach. She was applying a dab of lipstick when she heard footfalls on the cobbles under the window, and the gay drawl of American voices answered by a throaty laugh.

Alexis! Calling on Barry with her friends the Vanhusens!

For a moment a feeling of blind panic swept through Domini. She stood rigid and saw reflected in the mirror the sudden pallor of her face.

Then in blind haste she snatched up her bag and jerked open the bedroom door. Perhaps she could get downstairs before Barry let Alexis and her friends into the cottage. It wouldn't look so bad if she were downstairs with him . . .

Domini hadn't bargained on the fact that Barry had fallen into the country habit of leaving his front door on the latch . . . Alexis had entered the cottage with the freedom of someone who came often and she was half-way along the passage, the Vanhusens following, as Domini came running down the stairs.

Alexis stood stock still, with Domini poised above her on the third step with her hand clenching the stair rail.

"Well," Alexis drawled, "what are *you* doing here?"

Domini was too dry-mouthed to speak, and with a certain relief she heard Barry say: "Mrs. Stephanos has been having a look round my painting lair." His eyes met Domini's over Alexis smooth dark head, and her relief was shortlived as she saw how hard and reckless he looked—as though about to add that they were in love and Paul Stephanos could do what he darn well liked about it.

140

No! Her eyes shot an agonised message into his. Please, Barry, not like this!

"If there's nothing you like very much up in the studio, then I'd better let you have the painting that first took your eye," he drawled, a twist to his mouth.

She didn't quite take in his meaning, and it wasn't until they were all in the sitting room and he handed her his painting of the beach-after-storm that she came out of the daze into which panic had plunged her.

"You—didn't really want to sell this one," she managed.

"You're darn tooting he didn't," laughed Mr. Vanhusen. "I've been trying to persuade him to sell it for the past fortnight, and now you come along with your pretty face and he sells without a murmur of pain."

Alexis touched a ruby fingernail to the painting. "Eve could always persuade Adam to do *anything*, Milo," she said in her throaty voice. "You have a bargain there, Domini. What do you intend to do with it?"

"Mrs. Stephanos wants it as a present for her husband," Barry put in. "Now what are you all going to have to drink?"

Domini got away after about twenty minutes. It had stopped raining and she assured Milo Vanhusen that she would pick up a carriage-cab down by the market-place and that he had no need to drag himself away from the party in order to run her home.

The horse-drawn cab swayed and bumped up the gradient that led to the house of Paul's aunt. Barry had wrapped brown paper round the painting, covering it up as he had reluctantly covered up her presence at his cottage by saying she had gone there in search of a gift for Paul. But had Alexis been fooled by that excuse? Domini doubted it. She knew with a sinking heart that she had looked as guilty on those stairs leading down from Barry's room as only the innocent can look in a compromising situation.

Alexis had a weapon with which to make a lot of mischief, and the only way to stop her, Domini knew, was to fight as subtly as she would.

Domini gave a cold little shiver. She and Barry had been so right together, so happy and unspoiled. Now it was no longer right for them to be alone together.

Domini had never used calculation or guile in her dealing with Paul, and that evening she was driven to it to protect Barry rather than herself.

The gown she was wearing for the party was of Veronese velvet in orchid-blue. There was a long concealed zipper at the back of the dress, and she called Paul from the bathroom to assist her. He came through the open door carrying her corsage of wild white roses which he had stood in water to keep fresh. As he had dried the stems a thorn had pierced his hand and Domini saw that several of the petals were rubied as he laid the spray on the dressing-table. He came behind her to zip the dress, and she felt his lean hand against her waist as he closed the zip. The glowing material enclosed her as in a sheath, leaving her shoulders white and bare.

"Just wear the roses," Paul's warm lips brushed her shoulder. "Their whiteness matches your skin, my Sabine."

"Will you pin them on for me?" She stood very still as he did so, tall in front of her, dark and striking in his evening clothes.

"I've marked them with my blood." There was a strange smile on his mouth. "Shall I pull off the petals?"

"No, leave them." Her eyes met his, then she took hold of his hand and examined it in case the thorn had penetrated. "Rose thorns can poison," she said, speaking low, aware of his eyes upon her hair.

"Well," his tone of voice was droll, "will I die?"

"Not this time." She let go of his hand and turned to the mirror to take in her reflection. She wore no jewellery with the blue velvet dress, only the roses, close-furled in feathers of fern. Paul was reflected behind her bare shoulders in the mirror, and as she took in his dark, forbiddingly good-looking face and thought of him as he could look in anger, she reached forward quickly and opened the drawer in which lay Barry's painting.

"I bought you a present this morning, Paul." She turned to him and held it out. "I hope you like it. Milo Vanhusen was interested in buying it off Barry Sothern, but I got in ahead of him."

Paul stripped the brown paper from the canvas and studied the painting. His face was impassive for several long moments, and Domini could feel her heart beating very fast under his roses.

"My dear," he said at last, "you should not spend your money on me."

"Don't you like the painting?" She felt bitter with herself for the deception; down in the market that morning it had not occurred to her for one moment to buy Paul a present.

"I find the painting interesting." His eyes held hers. "I have seen it hanging on the wall at Sothern's cottage, and he once told me that he would never sell it because it was personal to him."

Paul paused there and Domini's heart felt clutched by sudden apprehension.

He flicked a finger at the painting. "Do you know what Sothern told me? That this was a representation of the conflict between what he wanted to give to his art, and what he felt for a certain woman. Domini," Paul's voice had gone low, almost menacing, "you are no stranger to the man who painted this, are you? You knew each other in England!"

Domini stood mesmerised by her husband's eyes . . . tiger eyes glittering in his proud, pagan face. She knew fear of him, and cold wonderment that Barry could let her give Paul the painting when he knew it would reveal their secret.

"Are you going to deny an association with Sothern in England?" Paul's voice was cold and clipped, the tips of his fingers bone white from gripping the frame of the painting.

"We were a boy and a girl on a beach," she said quietly. "If we were in love, it was an innocent love."

"Is it still an *innocent* love?" Paul looked cold, stern.

"*Yes.*" She tossed back her head in scorn at his question. "The Domini Dane whom Barry knew was left behind in England when I married you. She was someone you never knew, Paul. Someone you would not have wanted, for her hair was sea-tangled more often than not, and she thought it the height of romance to sit under the stars on the keel of an old boat, listening to a young man spilling out his ambitious heart. She didn't know, then, that ambition is the greater part of men, and love to them but a hunger of the body."

She heard Paul draw in his breath, but whatever he was about to say was held back as someone tapped on their door and opened it. Kara's gamin head came poking round it. "I have come to cadge some of that glamorous perfume you were wearing last night, Domini." She smiled from her sister-in-law to Paul and came into the room. Her hair was seal-glossy from an energetic brushing, and she wore a simple dress of linden-green. Covering her earlobes were the little silver lyres which Domini had bought her that morning.

"You look as pretty as a nymph tonight, Kara." Domini's hand shook a little as she sprayed scent over the girl, who cocked her head at Paul and studied his stern face.

"What is the matter with you?" she asked. "You look as though about to bring down the mountains on someone. Not darling Domini, surely?"

"Don't be such a child," he said curtly, and setting aside the painting he strode from the room, leaving Kara looking at Domini with distressed eyes.

"Is he angry with you because of this morning?" she asked.

"Men get angry, Kara." Domini touched the girl's cheek and managed a smile. "Shall we go downstairs? The party guests must be arriving."

"The party is for you and Paul," Kara said, "and he goes to it with a face like a thundercloud. What has happened, *kyria*?"

"Merely a quarrel between a wife and her husband," Domini forced a laugh, "so there's no need to make a Greek tragedy out of it."

But the party that night couldn't help but hold, for Domini, the elements of tragedy.

Tomorrow she and Paul would go home to their house on the eagle's crag, and her future with him loomed as cloudbound as the crag was said at times to be. Kara would be joining them at the house in a fortnight's time.

Paul's aunt had not been opposed to the idea of Kara staying with them, but she had been firmly of the opinion that her nephew and his bride should have *time alone* in their house before sharing it with his sister.

Domini gazed at the costumed Greek dancers who were entertaining at the party, and unaware her fingers crushed the white roses Paul had pinned above her heart. He stood alone across the lamplit patio, the leaves of a laurel tree casting shadows across his face that was taut as a Greek mask, immobile but for the tiger gleam of his eyes between his lashes.

In the shadow-play of the leaves his face was as Domini remembered it the night of the fire in Athens, and under her crushing fingers the petals of his roses fell one by one.

CHAPTER TWELVE

PAUL did not work at all that first week. Their days were spent down on the secluded beach below the black cliffs, and in the blue Ionian waters. They swam, and sailed a small painted caique, the sun on his naked brown shoulders as they moved rhythmically to the pull of the tiller.

It seemed to Domini, during these days and nights alone with Paul, that he meant to crush out every memory she had ever shared with Barry, or anyone else.

From the side of the caique she dived into the spray, while the sun ran in long fingers across the sea, as though playing a great harp. She rolled over lazily, watching Paul in the boat, wide shoulders outlined against the sun, a dark scrolling of curls at the bronzed nape of his neck. Something shot through her body and she began to swim towards the beach. She blinked the water out of her eyes, her hands raised to squeeze it from her hair as she ran up the sands towards the shade of the grotto where their picnic basket was tucked out of the sun.

She was slicing ice-cold *peponi* as Paul vaulted the side of the beached boat and came up the sands towards her. Under her lashes she watched him in his sailcloth trousers, bared from his waist to his throat like a Delphi bronze.

"I am ready for that." He threw himself down beside her and took a slice of the melon from her hand. His white teeth sank into the golden fruit, while Domini nibbled hers, bare toes in the warm supple sand.

An eagle swooped above the cliffs, wings stretched, gaunt neck thrust forward. Paul put back his arrogant head in order to watch the flight of the big dark bird.

His smile flashed as he took in the seven-foot span of the eagle wings. "Wonderful," he murmured, "just as in the proverb. Do you know it, Domini?"

She shook her head, thinking him as untamed and ruthless as any eagle in search of prey.

"The proverb quotes several wonders," he smiled. "Among them that of an eagle in the air, a ship in the midst of the sea . . . and a man with a maid."

"How interesting," she said. "Will you have a meat patty?" She leant away from him over the food basket, and his hand bit into her waist before slipping away.

"Yes, feed the brute," he crisped, "then he will sleep for an hour and you can enjoy yourself in the rockpools looking at the coloured fishes and searching for coralline."

She flushed at the sarcasm in his voice and handed him a patty rich with meat, along with a carton of spicy yoghourt and several large tomatoes. He sank back on his elbow and ate his lunch with his shielded eyes brooding on the sea. Domini poured coffee from the flask and added the wild honey which Paul liked. He took the cup and raised it to her. "Stin iyia sou," he said in Greek.

"To your health, Paul," she responded, and looked away from him as she drank her coffee and ate her lunch. Her health was important to him for only one reason—she believed he wanted her to have a child.

Their lunch finished and the basket tidied up, she left his side to sport in one of the rockpools where the tiny fish were rainbow-tinted, angel-winged, swimming in and out between her fingers like little puffs of breath. Paul had stretched out on the sand some yards from where she amused herself, the sun on his back and his face resting on his crossed arms. She wasn't sure whether he snoozed or lay there with the deceptive laziness of a replete and sun-warmed tiger.

Domini fingered some pebbles pale and smooth as a child's milk teeth, and she still smouldered at the high-handed way Paul had sent back Barry's painting.

"I don't care for it in my house," he had said. "You must think of something else to give me, my dear."

And last night, furious with him, she had given herself the satisfaction of locking her door on him. She had lain tense, listening to his movements in the adjoining room, but he didn't try her door and she finally fell asleep and awoke to the sound of Lita opening the curtains.

Lita wasn't a woman who smiled a great deal, but a smile touched her mouth as she gazed down at Domini with her hair warmly rich as honey of the wild hills, glowing against the pillows, and her skin pale-honeyed in contrast to the blue chiffon of her nightdress.

"How the sun comes bursting through the windows," said Domini, as she sat up and watched Lita pour out her morning tea.

"These are the rich-weather days for the island, madame," Lita said. "The grapes grow ripe and dark on the vine, and the hills are full of kids and lambs."

"Were you born on the island, Lita?" Domini asked, sipping her hot, sweet tea.

Lita stood holding the rococo teapot, with nymphs, elves and birds flying all over it. She inclined her head and her coiled hair was sloe-dark as the sun touched it. "I am from the hills, madame, a place of bandits in the old days, and wild legends. You know, of course, that I have Romany blood in my veins?"

Domini nodded, always intrigued by Lita's air of being in touch with the hidden things of life.

"The island was invaded during the war, madame, when I was a girl," she said. "The olive groves were strafed, the little farms burned, the girls taken as though they were Sabines."

Domini gave a shiver as she gazed at her maid, and Lita added quickly: "I was fortunate. My grandfather hid all our family in a cave in the hills, and my father and my brothers fought as partisans. But it did not end there for Greece. Came the rebellion and again the blunt thud of bullets in Greek earth and flesh and vine."

"It must have been a sad and terrible time for all of you," Domini said gently.

"But now it is ended." Lita smiled in her grave way. "Now here on the island the people have work and peace and enough food to eat. Madame, will you have a *beignet?*"

She held out the plate and Domini took a crumbly, delicious cake drenched in fine white sugar.

"*Kalo ya to stomacha,*" Lita smiled.

"They do indeed taste good. Do you know, Lita, I'm beginning to love Greek food." Domini gave a little laugh, as though surprised at herself. "Your island air must be good for the appetite."

Lita cast a shrewd look at her young mistress, then she picked up Domini's empty teacup and peered into it.

"Do you see a happy day ahead for me, Lita?" Domini's lashes quivered as she took a quick look at the door she had locked against Paul last night.

Lita frowned as she studied the tea-leaves. "There is to be an upheaval," she muttered. "I see it plainly."

"A storm?" Domini spoke wryly.

"Something not good is going to happen, madame." Lita's voice had sharpened. "It will happen today—"

There she broke off as a hand rattled the knob of that locked door. She turned to look, and again the knob was impatiently turned and rattled. Domini had the grace to blush as she met Lita's shocked eyes. "Unlock the door, Lita," she said, and the sharp click of the key in the lock seemed to add emphasis to the sudden tension in that large, sun-filled room.

Lita wished the master good morning, and then hurriedly departed. Domini sat slender and rather white-faced against her pillows, gazing across the room at him. He wore a dark silk shirt over grey slacks, and his eyebrows were joined in a forbidding ridge as he gestured curtly at the door Lita had just unlocked.

"Do that again, my girl," he crisped, "and I shall not wait like a lackey for your maid to let me into your august presence. *I shall kick the door down.*"

He looked angry enough to do it, and Domini's nervousness had the perverse effect of making her want to giggle. She put up a hand and bit at her knuckles as he came to the side of her bed, walking with all the grace and menace of a big cat. He stood looking down at Domini and as she saw his glance travel from her shoulders to the blue chiffon covering her bosom, she caught at the silk bedspread and drew it against her. He lifted an eyebrow at the action, and then he gave an unkind laugh that showed his white teeth.

"Locked doors and displays of maidenly virtue are likely to increase my ardour, not quench it," he drawled, and the next instant he was sitting on the side of the bed and gazing at her with cynical eyes. His lips twitched, whether with annoyance or amusement she couldn't really tell. His face was too baffling, too unreadable, while his strong dark proximity made her toes curl nervously together beneath the sheets.

Then with his tawny eyes upon the gold band on her left hand—the symbol of his ownership—he said curtly: "I am well aware, Domini, that you don't want me, but I am afraid you will have to tolerate my romantic lapses. However, you can console yourself with the thought that the day will surely come when I shall not need you any more."

He spoke the words with chilliness and irony, and Domini found herself flinching from him as though he had struck her. His words echoed and re-echoed in her mind, and their blatant honesty roused her to a blaze of stormy anger.

"I see, Paul," her eyes shot blue daggers at him. "you smashed my life just to satisfy a passing whim. You took my pride and bludgeoned me into marriage with you, just for the sake of possessing me for a few months. I always knew those were your reasons for marrying me, but I never thought you would have the gall and the cruelty to tell me outright.

"Well," her bosom lifted on a breath of anger shot with pain, "thanks for telling me. Now I shan't care that it's wrong to hate another person . . . I shall feel justified."

"Yes, feel yourself justified." He spoke almost lazily. "It is surprising how a feeling of justification eases the conscience."

"I doubt whether you have a conscience," she retorted. "I know you haven't a heart."

With a smile of irony he touched his hard-muscled chest, then with a shrug he leant over to the bed table and took hold of the book that lay there. He opened it and read a translated sentence or two of a masterly, earthy, colourful novel by Nikos Kazantzakis.

"Are you attempting to fathom the Greek personality?" Paul quirked an eyebrow at her.

"I read Kazantzakis for pleasure," she said coldly. "That, for me, is the main function of a novel."

"For each man is a prisoner within his own reactions to life and he cannot speak for everyone," Paul half-smiled. "Kazantzakis writes of love as though it were a sword slipping into the heart. Do you think he is right?"

"I wouldn't know," she shrugged.

"Yet you have loved, have you not, in a calflike way?" Paul said, his tawny eyes narrowing as he spoke.

"To fall in love is to hand yourself over to the whims

and possible cruelties of another person," she said icily. "I shall not risk that again."

Paul gestured at the door she had locked on him last night. "You did that because I sent back Sothern's painting," he said. "Not exactly a sign of indifference, eh?"

"Indifference towards whom?" Their eyes fenced, then Domini was borne back against her pillows as Paul leant towards her, bringing his darkly handsome face within an inch of her own. Her iris-blue eyes were filled with him, then his laugh feathered her mouth as he withdrew and got to his feet.

"I have to go and see someone this morning," he replaced her book on the bed table, "but I will join you later for an alfresco lunch down on the beach. I will give orders for a basket of food to be packed."

"As you please, Paul," she said, and watched him go from the room and close the door behind him. She put an arm across her eyes and lay very still for several minutes, but there were no tears in her. Her pain and bitterness went too deep for tears.

After a light Greek breakfast of coffee, rolls and honey, Domini took her book and made for a grape arbour that was tucked away in the garden, shadowy with vines and clustering bunches of small grapes not yet ripe. The cicadas were glazed hints in the green boughs of the pepper-trees and the umbrella-pines. Honeysuckle and junipers scented the air, and there were patches of irises blue as sapphires.

Domini sat in the arbour and buried herself in her novel with determination. Yannis came looking for her at about eleven o'clock, carrying the picnic lunch which Paul had ordered. The basket wasn't really heavy, but Yannis insisted on carrying it down to the beach. Domini liked this grave-eyed manservant of Paul's, who could name all the island birds and the wild flowers that grew in drifts beside the path they took to the beach. He and Lita were childless, and it seemed to Domini that in a way they regarded her as a child. They ran the house on the crag with such smoothness that there was little for Domini to do beyond exploring the big rooms and the winding stairways that led to lumber lofts.

"How beautiful and calm the island is this morning, Yannis." Domini paused on the down-winding path to take in the sheer blue of the Ionian, and the pearl-shot light of Greece shining on sea and sand and the water-silked rocks.

Yannis smiled as Domini stood looking about her, a light breeze playing with her hair, young and seemingly carefree in a halter-top and beach skirt.

"Oh, look at that, Yannis!" She pointed towards the lagoon where a sleek dolphin shot upwards as though on wings, and then went under in a show-off dive.

Domini was sun-basking when Paul joined her on the beach. She didn't hear him come across the sands, but felt the long shadow of him fall across her. He seemed to tower into the sun above her, proud and Apollo-like, not smiling. As she sat up and saw his face more clearly, it seemed to her that he looked a little weary.

"Do you want lunch right now?" she asked.

"Not if you don't. I thought we might go out in the caique for a while."

"Right you are." She jumped to her feet before he could assist her. Again her eyes flashed over his face; she realised that his head was aching and he hoped to assuage the pain in the sea-wind.

"Paul," she touched his arm with nervous fingers, "what do the doctors say about your bad heads?"

"My dear," his smile was mocking, his eyes unreadable behind his sunglasses, "are you actually concerned for me?"

"I don't like to see anyone in pain." She withdrew her hand from his arm as though stung. "Sorry if I'm intruding."

"The pain will go in a while." He strode to where the caique was beached, untied the rope that secured it to a bollard and pushed it down into the water. He tossed off his shirt, and as he swung Domini into the boat she felt his hard muscles against her. He held her a moment, recklessly smiling as a Greek pirate. "Sometimes, my little piece of plunder, I don't think you quite hate me," he murmured.

She stared up at him and was vividly conscious again of the things he had said that morning. "I'm making the best of a bad bargain," she said coolly, "now I know my sentence isn't a lifetime one."

He laughed and let her go. He swung to the tiller and headed the boat out to sea, and in a while the tangy salt-breezes and leaping dolphins were bringing the sparkle back to Domini's eyes. "How is your headache?" Domini shouted above the singing of the spray, and the snoring of their motor.

"Much better," he threw over his shoulder. "The dolphins are full of play, eh? Look at that bronze-blue fellow, he has his share of *pallikari.*"

The big dolphin was a little too daring and bold, for several times he rocked the boat, almost sending Domini toppling into the water. As she laughed and clutched the side, Paul warned her to be careful. "There are not only dolphins in these waters," he added.

He meant sharks, and he refused to let Domini dive in for a swim until they were safe inside the coralline reef of the lagoon, where the fish were too small to attract the fierce, greedy sea-tigers.

Domini stirred out of her abstraction by the rockpool, where she had been sitting so still, so absorbed in her thoughts, that the sand had dried to grits between her toes. She rose and was running towards the surf to wash them out when something stabbed the underside of her left foot and she gave a cry of pain.

She had stepped on a prickly sea-urchin and upon taking a look at her foot she saw that several dark spines had penetrated under the skin. Domini knew they would fester if not pulled out, and she sat down on a nearby boulder and tried to extricate them with her fingernails.

"What have you done?" Paul had come to her side.

"Oh," she glanced up through a tousled wing of hair, "I stepped on a sea-urchin and collected a few of his spines."

"Let me see." He knelt in front of her and took her small foot in his hand. After a moment he looked at her. "These will have to be taken out with tweezers, but if you walk on the foot they will go in deeper. Come, I will carry you to the house."

"Not up the cliffside, Paul!" She drew back from him, laughing nervously. "I've put on a little weight since coming to Greece."

"One ounce, or two?" he mocked. His arms came round her and he lifted her with easy strength against his naked chest, where his Greek medal was meshed in the triangle of crisp dark hair. Their eyes met as she lay in his arms, then his glance moved to her throat, where a nerve pulsed under her pale honey skin.

"Are you still so nervous in my arms, Domini?" he chided her. "You should be well used to them by now."

He trod sand cavernously and carried her across the beach and in under the arch of the cave that led to the house. The sea-green shadows enclosed them, and she could feel the strong beat of his heart like a touch against her breast. Suddenly, as in the caique an hour or more ago, her body felt weak, shot through with a knowledge not yet made clear to her mind. In the caique she had been able to escape over the side from Paul, but here in his arms she was held captive. The arrogant jut of his chin above her head was a warning that she lie still and let herself be borne like Undine to the castle.

The cave grew dimmer as they penetrated to the heart of it, and then like the growl of a hidden beast, there echoed above them, running along the damp stone walls, an ominous grumbling noise. Paul stood stock still, his arms tightening to bruising point about Domini.

"What is it, Paul?" Her hand tightened on his naked shoulder and her fingernails bit into him, unaware.

He didn't answer right away, but stood straining his ears, sparking as a cat does in the presence of sudden danger. Something cracked, the ground shuddered, and Paul dropped Domini to her feet and said urgently: "Run, child . . . there is going to be a cave-in!"

Her heart pounded as she ran. She knew they were only minutes away from the door that would release them from the danger of the cave into the grounds of the house. Again there was that awful cracking sound and Domini was looking up, horrified, as the cave roof opened and with a sound like coals through a hole the time-worn stone came tumbling down, throwing her to her knees . . . forcing a cry out of her that was quickly choked by a rush of dust and pain . . .

CHAPTER THIRTEEN

PAUL'S den was shadowy, its ceiling of carved juniper wood and plain white walls lending it a calm, monastic air that was not echoed by the man who paced the room, back and forth, tigerishly.

He had long since changed his torn and dusty trousers, and the lacerations on his hands had been treated by Yannis. The doctor was busy upstairs. He had been up there for hours, it seemed to Paul.

He crushed out his half-smoked cheroot and went out on the balcony that had only a delicate iron balustrade between the enclosure and a sheer drop to the rocks and the shiny dark sea. Overhead the sky was webbed with star-beams and there was a musky tang of pines hanging on the night air. Lamps moved like fireflies far down on the water, where men were night-fishing from their caiques.

Paul's gashed and iodined hands clenched on the balustrade. If this caused pain, he didn't appear to feel it. He waited, staring down at the sea which whispered as it met the rocks. The lamps on the drifting caiques were enticing the curious fish like moths to flame. They would be leaping blindly to the hook, struggling silver and slender as they were forced out of the sea to drown in the air.

Footfalls were deadened by the carpet covering the floor of the den, and Paul sensed rather than heard the man who came to the open window behind him. He swung round. His expression could not be seen, for the shadows were too dense. "Tell me!" The words lashed out in Greek. "How is she now, Metros?"

The Greek doctor came out on to the balcony. He cast a swift look at the flimsy barrier between Paul

Stephanos and the sheer cliffs that ended far down on back-breaking rocks.

"Come inside, Paul," he urged. "There we can talk better."

"What is it, Metros?" Paul gestured at the drop from the balcony. "Are you afraid I shall damn my soul completely? Domini is dead, eh? I knew it when I lifted that last rock and saw how still she lay—"

"We cannot talk out here!" Metros took hold of Paul's arm and drew him indoors. He closed the windows with a decisive slam, and pulled the curtains across them. "The lamp, man," he ordered. "The lamp!"

There was a click and the desk lamp was slanting light at an odd angle on to Paul's face, showing its taut cheekbones and the hollows beneath them. His scar was livid, its edges drawn and pulsing.

"Domini—" he caught his breath harshly. "She did not regain consciousness, did not ask for—anyone?"

"Your wife is not dead." The Greek doctor took up a decanter and filled a small glass, which he thrust into Paul's hand. "Drink that, my friend. Come."

Paul stared at the doctor, then with a jerk of his dark head he tossed back the brandy. Then with tousled hair and blue-shaded jaw he stood menacing the doctor with his tiger-eyes. "What did all that rock do to her?" he demanded. "Is she to be crippled? Is that it?"

The doctor had a kindly, haggard face under grey-streaked dark hair, and looking at Paul he tapped a cigarette against his case and slipped it between his lips. He struck a match, lit up and puffed a plume of smoke. "Your young and beautiful wife," he said quietly, "has lost the child."

"What?" Paul gazed at Metros, dumbfounded. "But I-I had no idea— a *child*? But she told me nothing—"

"She may not have been sure." Metros studied Paul

with dark, shrewd eyes. "A young bride, far from her own people, and the pregnancy was but two months along."

"Two months?" Paul seemed to look down the weeks to that first night with Domini; an intense sadness filled his eyes.

"I am sorry, Paul." Metros gave his arm a grip of sympathy. "For you this child would have meant much, I know that. But the girl will survive the loss and the severe bruising she has sustained. She can have other children—there is time."

"No!" Paul spoke harshly. "There will not be a second time. The child she would have loved is gone—gone like happiness, elusive, not to be found by us together."

"What a way for a man to talk!" Metros spoke angrily. "That girl must not be denied a child to love in place of—"

"Of me?" Paul said ironically. "My friend, that girl hates me, the very sight and sound and touch of me. Ah, you look shocked! But I assure you it is true. When you have lived side by side with that for almost two months—two months all but a few fleeting hours—you are in no doubt. It is a look in the eyes. A shrinking when I reach out to touch. A quaver in the voice as she holds on to the tears she was unacquainted with until she met me."

"The girl married you, Paul."

"You are a Greek, Metros." Paul's smile was a mere twist of the lips. "You know as well as I that love does not always enter into the marriage bargain for a woman."

"I—see." Dr. Demetrios Suiza stubbed his cigarette. "Would such a state of affairs have anything to do with your refusal to reconsider that other decision of yours, the one we discussed in my office earlier today?"

"Not really, Metros." Paul pulled away from his desk and stepped towards the door. "And now may I go up and see my wife?"

"She is under sedation, Paul, and will sleep until the morning. I have put her in the charge of that extremely capable woman, Lita, but naturally you may take a look at her." Metros came across to Paul and being several inches shorter he had to look up at him. "Get some sleep yourself, my friend. The girl is young, healthy. Very soon she will be well again."

"You will come again in the morning, Metros?"

"Of course."

"The damnable part is," Paul pushed a hand through black hair that was already standing on end, "if I had gone ahead of Domini in the cave, I would have taken the bulk of that rock fall. I told her to run ahead of me. I thought she would reach the door in time."

"You must not reproach yourself for that," Metros said as they went out into the hall, where he collected his black bag and his driving-jacket. They shook hands at the door, after which Paul went upstairs and quietly entered Domini's bedroom, where in a chair beside a muted lamp Lita was occupying her hands with some knitting.

Paul approached the bed, where Domini lay so small, so lost in drugged slumber after the ordeal of the rock fall and the subsequent loss of her child. Her lashes made dark fans on her cheek and her left hand was curled on the sheet, the wide band of gold looking too heavy for the slim finger that wore it.

The silence in the room was complete, uncanny, for Lita had ceased to move her knitting needles. Then Paul said quietly: "You may get some rest, Lita. I will stay here."

The woman hesitated, but it was plain from Paul's face that he had made up his mind on staying, so, after taking a look at Domini, Lita slipped out of the big, dim room with its faint smell of drugs. She did not go straight to bed, however, but made her way downstairs and brewed a pot of dark Turkish coffee for Paul. She added a plate of biscuits to the tray, then carried it upstairs to him. He had placed an armchair at the side of the bed and was sitting there, his eyes gleaming in the shadows like those of a watchful tiger. Lita placed the coffee tray within easy reach of his hand, then she left him alone with his sleeping wife.

The darkness was gradually lifting towards the east, and a fine steely line was cutting night from day when Domini stirred awake. She was vaguely aware that someone was with her, helping her to sit up a little so she could ease her dry throat with cool sips of lime juice. She felt oddly lightheaded, and she ached all over. Was this the 'flu again? she wondered.

"Thank you," she murmured, not quite certain who it was who made her pillows comfortable and who laid her down so carefully. Her weighted eyelids just wouldn't lift, but she had a vague impression of shoulders above her like wings. She was asleep before she could think who the person might be, and when next she awoke Lita was with her, along with a stocky, kind-eyed man who turned out to be a Dr. Demetrios Suiza.

Eight days later he discussed with her the miscarriage she had suffered. The shock of being half buried under the earth and rock of the cave-in had caused it, he said.

Domini sat very still against the cushions of the lounger on which she was resting. On the day of the accident she had had an elusive awareness of the child, but her mind had not been ready to accept the fact. Now it was too late to be pleased, or disquieted.

"Paul wished for a child," she said quietly. "He

162

must have been disappointed when you told him I had lost it."

"I am sure he would have been more concerned if he had lost you," the doctor said, and though his English was not as fluent as Paul's, Domini understood each polite and stilted word. She studied her hands on the lap of her silk robe, and the doctor watched her and marvelled at her composure. A Greek girl would have wept brokenly over losing her first child, but this cool and lovely English girl sat dry-eyed, seemingly unmoved. Metros Suiza thrust a cigarette between his lips and reflected that it was as Paul had said — this girl with the cool blue eyes and the regal young head was not in love with her husband.

They sat out on the *piazza,* where Turkish tea in tall glasses was brought to them by Yannis. There were also finely cut sandwiches with various fillings on the trolley, and a selection of pastries. Paul had gone down to his aunt's in the car; he was bringing Kara back with him.

"You must try a sandwich," Metros urged, as Domini sipped her tea and made no attempt to fill a plate. "Come, I will serve you."

"I'm not really hungry, doctor," Domini protested.

"But you must eat, my child, otherwise you will take longer to get well. There, a sandwich of chicken and another of paté. Very nourishing, and I insist that you eat every mouthful."

The doctor was too kind and friendly to be denied and Domini found herself eating the sandwiches and exchanging impressions of Greece with him. She also learned that he was a widower with one son who was at medical school in Athens.

"He will not be content to be a doctor on an island," Dr. Suiza smiled. "But me, I am suited here. I have my work at the children's clinic which your husband has endowed, and affluent patients like him help to make up for the shore folk who find it harder to meet their bills."

"Do you treat Paul for his headaches, Dr. Suiza?" Domini asked.

The doctor was choosing a pastry, his consideration of the delectable cakes a more ponderous one than the occasion seemed to demand. The fork was poised in his fingers for at least a minute, then as he made his selection he shot a look at Domini under bristling brows. "Has Paul talked to you about his—headaches?" he asked.

"Not really. It seems to rattle him if I bring up the subject," she said. "Being so strong apart from the headaches, I suppose he hates to admit to a weakness."

"Perhaps." The doctor forked pastry into his mouth, and was intently watching the bees at their honey-plunder in a nearby mesh of wall-trailing flowers.

"Paul is very much a Greek," Metros said suddenly. "And Greeks are never easy of understanding. They are like icebergs, one might say, with more of them in the depths than is showing."

"Icebergs can cause a lot of damage," Domini murmured.

"But they can melt—ice is not iron."

"I imagine it would take considerable heat," Domini laughed.

The doctor smiled at the sound, and the sudden vivid loveliness which laughter brought to the face he had seen only in pain, and in cool composure. His eyes lit up. He saw now that he had been wrong to think her cool—ah, how those eyes of hers reflected the blue of sea and sky, and what a delicious curve there was to her mouth. She was but a child really, sensitive, shy, not the sort to show her feelings openly.

He leant forward and looked directly at her. "There is one flame that can consume everything," he said.

164

"There is very little that can withstand its full force."

"Is this a riddle, Dr. Suiza?" she smiled.

"One might indeed call it a riddle, my child. The most complex in the world, and not really fathomed even after all the years since Eve first handed the forbidden apple to Adam."

"I see." Her hands came together as though seeking comfort of each other. "You are talking about love, doctor."

"Do you not agree that it is a fascinating subject, madame?"

She glanced away from him and wondered for a wild moment if in her pain and delirium she had revealed herself to him. He was kind, mature, he reminded her a little of Uncle Martin, but to confide in another was only a temporary relief followed by embarrassment, regret at having lowered your guard.

"I wonder why the apple was forbidden?" he murmured. "If Eve had not been daring enough to pluck it, even Eden would have been a rather dull place."

"She and her husband were banished from Eden," Domini reminded the doctor.

"Would you not say that they found another that was far more exciting?" he chuckled. "Come, to play like children in a garden is fun, but to enter a jungle and to live every fraught and unexpected moment—why, that is *living*."

Domini looked at the doctor then, and the shrewd glint in his eye told her that he *did* know something. She and Barry had played like children in a garden . . . had she mentioned Barry during those dark hours following the cave-in?

Dr. Suiza got to his feet, announcing with reluctance that he had some more patients to visit. When he took Domini's hand, he gave it a meaning squeeze. "We must talk together again," he smiled. "Soon, eh? When you feel ready?"

"What about, doctor?" she asked, not quite sure she understood him.

"About the things we cannot escape from, my child. The inevitable things, like birth, love—and death."

She gazed at him, wide-eyed, lost. His dark eyes held hers, then he bent his grey-streaked head and kissed her hand. He wished her goodbye in Greek and half a minute later the *piazza* was empty but for herself. She sat very still, in the grip of an acute sense of loneliness. The house beyond the windows of the *piazza* was very quiet, for this was siesta time, when even the birds seemed to snooze in the branches of the trees.

Domini leaned back against a cushion and closed her eyes. The pine trees rustled, the sea whispered, and her dead baby seemed to tug at her heart. Gone was the love he would have brought and given, and a tear stole down Domini's cheek.

She slept for a short while, and awoke suddenly to a sense of coldness. The sun was no longer shining on to the *piazza,* and Domini saw that during her nap the haze that had overhung the sea for most of the day had crept inland and formed a belt around the headland and the house.

Domini had been warned to expect these fogs, but she had had no idea they could shroud this end of the island so suddenly, so completely. A trifle unnerved, she slipped off the lounger and went to the end of the *piazza* to look down over the cliffs to the sea. She could barely perceive it, though far below she could hear the hollow lap of the water on the rocks. Slow curls of mist drifted up to form in globules on her hair, and she had an empty sensation of being suspended with the house in the clouds.

She heard footfalls, a man's, but when she glanced around it was Yannis who was coming towards her. "We seem to be cut off up here, Yannis!" she exclaimed.

"Yes, madame." He nodded gravely. "It is very damp out here—you should come indoors."

"Yes, I am coming indoors, Yannis." She felt warmed by his concern for her. "Up here I feel rather like Helen walking the ramparts of Troy — will the fog last long, do you think?"

"Several hours, I would say, madame."

"Oh—then that might delay my husband and his sister. Do you think it might? That is a steep and twisting road leading up here—with visibility cut down by the fog I don't suppose Paul would chance driving home until it clears, not with Kara as a passenger."

"I doubt it, madame." Yannis held open the door of the *salotto* and Domini entered the large room, pooled with shadows, warmed where a logwood fire burned orange-bright.

"You pet, Yannis, you lit a fire!" Domini caught at the silk folds of her robe and hurried to the glow. Still bruised and stiff, she couldn't curl down as she liked to on the big, dark bearskin rug, so she sat down instead in Paul's winged chair and held her hands to the warmth of the crackling logs. Lita was preparing a special meal to greet Kara, but as it seemed only too likely they would be delayed by the fog, Domini told Yannis that she would have a snack here by the fire at about seven o'clock. She added that she hoped Lita wouldn't mind delaying the main meal.

He smiled and shook his head. "Our pleasure is that you are well again," he murmured. "Would you like a cup of English tea right now, madame?"

"Mmm." She nodded gratefully, her eyes misty with tears as she watched Yannis go from the room. Greek kindness, so utter, so without any motive but that of wanting to ease a burden. Domini had to blink hard, for in that moment she could have given way completely to the tears banked about her heart.

Her cup of tea was lovely, there by the fire, with her feet slipped out of her mules and her toes buried in the fur of the bearskin rug. The fog had stolen closer to the windows, and the firelight gleamed on the dark-wood surfaces, and lit to red the stone frieze of flute-players, centaurs, and maidens with torches. An antique loving-cup on a side table shone in the shadows, and there was the topaz gleam of foot-crushed wine in a flagon of crystal. All that was needed was the soft, cosy purr of a cat.

In a while a little carved clock chimed the hour and Domini decided to go upstairs and put on a dress. She felt tired, achy, but was determined not to go to bed. The fog would clear in a while, and it would be more of a cosy greeting for Kara and Paul to find her awaiting them.

She put on a blue dress with long sleeves, for Kara would be distressed enough about the results of the accident without seeing the bruises on Domini's arms. Her reflected face in the mirror was pale, with crescents of shadow still outlining her eyes, and she applied make-up to hide the ravages—fading now, thank goodness!

Um, the dress looked a little plain and needed a neck-lace to brighten it up. Domini opened the drawer in which she kept her jewellery—and there in place of the plain leather case was a filigree box carved all over with delightful imps and fauns, fishes and shells, and birds on the wing. Domini opened the box—yes, her jewellery was inside, arranged in a nest of artful little drawers.

The antique jewel-box was a gift from Paul. A silent token of his sympathy, she supposed, for not once in the past eight days had he mentioned the loss of the child. His manner, in fact, had been curiously withdrawn.

She touched the intricate carving of his gift, aware of a tactile pleasure that did not penetrate her heart. She took out the simple row of pearls that had been her mother's and as she clipped them on she thought of her wedding day. Pearls were unlucky for a bride, but she had expected tears for every pearl that day and it hadn't seemed to matter that she was challenging fate.

On her way downstairs she paused at the lyre window at the bend of the gallery and saw that the fog was still impenetrable. There was a ghostly rattle of leaves and boughs from the direction of the pine woods, and the house felt hollow and empty. She was glad to find Yannis in the *salotto,* drawing the curtains with a cosy swish, swish. The lamps were alight, and a log turned over with a hiss of resin and flames.

Tension seemed to lose the sharp edge of its talons in the warmth and cosiness of this room, and Domini fingered with a smile the spray of flowers that Yannis had placed on the small table set for one beside the fireplace. He had switched on the radio and *Les Sylphides* came in gentle waves across the fog-bound sea from Athens.

"Does the fog seem any thicker, Yannis?" Domini slipped into the chair he drew out for her.

"I would say it is about the same, madame." He poured her a fluted glass of wine . . . the Cretan wine that Paul always said should be taken with wild figs and honey-cakes, for no love supper of old had ever been complete without them.

She gave a little shiver as she seemed to hear his laughter, and warmed herself with a sip of the wine.

"I am sure Monsieur Stephanos will not attempt driving home in the fog, madame." Yannis scattered juniper needles on to the burning logs and their scent wafted out like an incense. "Now I will bring the soup."

169

Domini ate the meal to please Yannis and his wife rather than out of appetite, and the table had been taken away and she was drinking her coffee, seated in Paul's winged chair, when there were several loud knocks on the front door. Domini's heart beat with agitation, and she was standing up when the door of the *salotto* burst open and Nikos Stephanos came hurrying in . . . followed by tall, blond Barry Sothern.

CHAPTER FOURTEEN

NIKOS, his black hair damply curled by the fog. made straight to Domini and caught at her hands. Her hands were cold and trembly in his, she knew something awful had happened — Paul and Kara had had an accident in the car coming home. Her eyes flashed to Barry, as though in appeal, then she said to Nikos:

"It's Kara and Paul, isn't it? They crashed in the car?"

Nikos bit his lip, while Barry jammed his hands down hard in the pockets of his driving jacket. The collar was up about his hair, mussing it, and his eyes looked very dark as they met Domini's.

"Tell me!" Her fingernails bit into the backs of Nikos' hands.

"Kara is all right," he said. "Paul—he has been taken to hospital—"

Domini's breath caught sharply. "Has he been badly hurt?"

Nikos shot a look at Barry, then he pressed Domini down into a chair, while Barry strode over to the cabinet on which stood decanters. There came a clink as he removed a stopper, assured himself that the container held brandy and poured out a peg. As he came back across the room with it, Nikos said to Domini: "There has not been a car crash. Paul has been taken ill—very critically ill—"

"Drink this, honey." Barry put a warm hand over her shoulder and the rim of the glass to her lips. She drank, knowing that he gave her brandy because Nikos was about to add something worse to what he had already told her.

He stood looking down at her, his young face pale and distressed above the black rolled collar of his sweater. "My cousin is not expected to live," he said huskily. "The doctors have given him only a few hours, and I thought you would like to be with him, Domini."

Paul was dying? She glanced up at Nikos, unbelievingly.

"It would not have been right for you to hear such news over the telephone," he went on, distressed and not quite sure what one said on occasions like this. "Barry was at the house, so we came together here in the car. The fog was bad lower down the slopes, but it is a little clearer now——"

Fog, Domini thought dazedly. What did the fog matter?

She jumped to her feet and saw Yannis hovering anxiously in the doorway; it was plain from his face that he had overheard what Nikos had said about Paul. He was shaking his head to himself as he went to fetch her coat and scarf, the beautiful ocelot into which Barry helped her, buttoning it for her and pulling the big collar up about her head, which she swathed in the silk scarf she had bought off a pedlar in the Plaka—— the stepped Plaka which she had explored with Paul . . .

Paul—dying!

She found herself installed in the car with Barry seated beside her on the back seat. Yannis and Lita stood in the doorway of the house, watching quiet as ghosts as Nikos swung the car to face the fog-bound gradient. Lita's head was swathed in a dark shawl and her eyes were wet.

Domini's were quite dry, but they felt as though they were burning in her head, as if she had been peering through a fog for a long while and was at last beginning to see a little clearer.

Paul had known for months that this illness was

coming on him—those headaches had been his warning, and his reason for some of the things he had done, and said.

Paul had known for a long while that he was going to die!

Domini felt Barry's hand close in warm comfort about hers. The car was making slow progress down the gradient, moving forward for a few yards, then coming almost to a halt as Nikos felt the wheels on the grass at the edge of the steep road. Driving here with Paul the other night, the car had seemed to hang suspended in the stars—like Apollo's chariot. Now there wasn't a star to be seen, only the wandering mist and the wraith-like shapes of trees.

In a while Nikos told them over his shoulder that he had glimpsed the circling beacon of the lighthouse mid-way between Andelos and a neighbouring island. This meant that they were nearing the harbour, and the hospital.

Domini's heart beat with the quick, heavy stroke of physical and mental tension. She was leaning against Barry's shoulder, grateful for his strong, silent company. What was he thinking as he sat quietly holding her hand? That fate was winding in a little more of the cord, binding them close again as the life ebbed out of the man who had come between them?

"What happened, Barry?" Her tight throat had un-locked. "Were you at Aunt Sophula's house when—when Paul was taken ill?"

"I had been out sailing with the Vanhusens—and Alexis," he explained. "The fog began to thicken, so we headed back into harbour. Alexis and I had a drink at the Vanhusens' place, then I walked her home as the fog had grown pretty dense. We arrived at her house just as the ambulance was leaving with Paul. Kara and her aunt went with him. Nikos was at the house to explain the situation to us—Alexis and myself."

"Poor little Kara must have been very upset," Domini murmured, picturing the distress of the girl who adored Paul.

"She went with him without tears." Nikos was peering intently through the half moons made by the windscreen wipers. "She seemed suddenly grown up."

No tears, Domini thought, for the Greeks who cry for joy and face sternly the anguish in their hearts. All the same, it was a good thing that Kara had Nikos to turn to.

Their journey through the fog to the hospital took almost two hours, but at long last they were pulling into the forecourt of the building and Nikos was helping Domini to alight from the car. The three of them walked across to the entrance, where a uniformed attendant directed them to the staircase that led to the floor on which Monsieur Stephanos' private room was situated. "Do you want me to come up with you?" Barry said to Domini. She nodded, and it wasn't until the three of them were mounting the stairs that she noticed she was still wearing her flat-heeled Greek slippers. They were gaily embroidered, incongruous against the sombre stone stairs.

The corridor was dimly lit. Paul's room was about halfway down, and as they neared the door a nurse came out, carrying a small instrument tray covered by a white cloth. Nikos went up to her and asked if the patient's wife could go in to see him. The nurse turned to Domini and said something to her, but she spoke in Greek and Nikos had to explain that Madame Stephanos was English. He then informed Domini of what the nurse had said, that the doctors were with Paul at the moment and would they please join the other relatives in the waiting-room. The nurse pointed it out to them, a room with glazed doors a few yards farther along the corridor.

There they found Kara and her aunt. Kara jumped to her feet and came running to Domini; her eyes were like a stricken fawn's, dark and hurt and bewildered. "Oh, Domini," she said helplessly. "What shall we do without Paul?"

Domini took hold of the girl and hugged her close. She had no answer for Kara, no answer for herself.

They waited, not speaking much, while the clock ticked persistently on the wall and the density of the fog slowly cleared to leave a hazy midnight sky. A young nurse came in with steaming cups of coffee on a tray, and Domini was clasping her cup and trying to warm her hands with it when the door opened again and the nurse they had first seen came into the waiting-room. She beckoned to Domini and when Kara jumped up as well, the nurse said regretfully that only the wife of Monsieur Stephanos was to be allowed to see him at the moment.

Kara, holding on sternly to her self-control, took Domini's half-finished cup of coffee and said huskily: "Go to him, *kyria*. It is your right."

Domini followed the nurse to Paul's sickroom, and she didn't notice when she first entered that a man in medical white was standing quietly in the shadows by the window. Domini walked slowly to the side of the white bed, where Paul lay very still, his eyes closed, his black hair in pain-damp scrolls along his forehead. Pain of an indescribable nature had set its mark on his face, leaving it fine-drawn and shadowed. Very gently Domini touched his cheek and felt the taut bone. He didn't move. Her touch was not felt, for he had gone beyond all awareness of her.

She didn't hear the doctor as he came across to her, but sensing a presence she turned her head and met the kind, shrewd eyes of Metros Suiza.

"It seems so wrong to see Paul lying so helpless," she murmured. "Doctor," she gripped his arm, "can't anything be done? Have we got to stand by and see him— *die?*"

Dr. Suiza studied her for a long moment, then he took her hand and led her out of the room, into which the waiting nurse slipped at once. Dr. Suiza led Domini down the corridor, away from the waiting-room and into a consulting-room. He closed the door very firmly and told her to sit down. She did so, wearily, and faced him across the desk.

"What is it that's killing my husband?" she said painfully.

"A fraction of metal," Metros said quietly. "A splinter from a grenade that exploded in his face when as a mere boy he fought in the rebellion that tore his beloved Greece in two."

"But it happened so long ago," Domini protested. "How could he have gone on all these years—?"

"Stranger things have been known, my dear, and that destructive fraction of metal might have lain undetected, giving him little trouble at all—but for a certain incident that occurred just under two years ago. You know that Paul had a brother?"

She felt the dilation of her eyes as they locked with the doctor's. "Loukas died of drowning almost two years ago," she said. "Paul went undersea to try to save him."

"Quite so." Metros inclined his head. "And upon coming to the surface he suffered a prolonged blackout. We thought it advisable to detain him in hospital in case of complications, and it was during those few days that we made tests and discovered that during his act of re-surfacing on an inadequate supply of air that splinter of metal had shifted under the pressure and re-located itself in a far more dangerous section of the brain. From the moment that shifting took place, Domini, your husband began to live on borrowed time."

"You—told him of this?" Domini asked, a hand at her hurting throat.

"Paul Stephanos is not a man from whom you can keep the truth." Metros shrugged, his faint smile was tinged with sadness and admiration. "A brave *andarte* at sixteen turns into quite a man as the years go by. A bold, daring man, who has too much respect for the earthy truths of life to be fobbed off with weak fabrications. The headaches began almost at once. Acute agony which drugs help—but not always."

Domini sat very still, recalling the times when Paul had withdrawn alone into his shell of pain. She had felt compassion for him—God help her—but stubborn pride had kept her from going to the tiger who wanted to be alone to lick his wounds.

A hard, tearless sob broke in her throat. "Can nothing be done?" she cried across the desk at Dr. Suiza. "Surely this metal splinter could be removed by surgery? Paul has money. He could afford the cleverest of brain surgeons—"

"I quite agree." Metros leant towards her, his hands gripped together. "There is an operation that could save him, and without it he will die as surely as morning must come. He will go out with one of the tides, unless a surgeon removes within the next few hours what is killing him—to give him dark life for even darker death!"

Domini stared at Metros, her heart in her throat. "Dark life?" she whispered. "Blindness?"

"Blindness certainly, but whether or not it would be total we are not sure." Metros got to his feet and came to lean on the desk near Domini's chair. His face looked haggard, but his eyes seemed to hold small leaping flames that burned into Domini's. "I have begged Paul to be sensible and undergo the operation, but he shrinks from the horror of being blind and a possible burden to the people he has always cared for and protected—little Kara, and now yourself, my dear."

"Oh, why didn't he tell me?" Domini whispered, half to herself.

"He is not a man to want pity," Metros said quietly. "He is strong; he has the heart of a tiger. But for a Greek to face the awful prospect of blindness is worse than death itself. Have you not noticed how Greeks love to be out in the Grecian sun from early morning to the fall of dusk? Have you not seen how they keep darkness out of their houses with many lights at night? Paul is all Greek. He has chosen to die rather than live in the dark."

"But he can't die!" Domini clutched at the edge of the desk. "What would we do without him—Kara and I—and all the other people here on the island who care for him so much?"

"Do you realise what you have just said, my dear?" Metros quietly smiled.

She nodded, her eyes brimming with tears above the hand she crushed against her pain-wrenched mouth. "He must have that operation," she whispered fiercely. "I-I can sign for it, can't I, Dr. Suiza? That is the right of a wife?"

"Very much the right of a wife!" Metros strode round the desk and snatched up the telephone; his eyes held hers, very fiery and Greek. "Have you the courage to face Paul — a live and threshing tiger of a Paul—in, say, a week from now?"

She was standing up, head high against the collar of her ocelot coat, her eyes very blue and stinging with tears. "He can kill me if he wishes," she said with spirit. "Where's that form I have to sign, doctor?"

"First I am putting through a call to Athens." He rapidly dialled a number. "The Graces have been good enough to lift the fog, now let us pray that the surgeon we need is free to take a plane at a moment's notice."

Domini closed her eyes and silently prayed, while Metros Suiza crackled Greek into the mouthpiece of the phone.

The grounds of the hospital were damp with the dews of dawn. Small opals of moisture clung to blades of grass and the furled petals of a mass of morning-glory. The early birds were chattering away, and the rising sun was firing with gold the tops of the trees. After the fog of yesterday it was going to be a lovely day, as Domini saw from the window of the hospital room she had shared through the night with Kara.

Kara still slept. Nikos had taken his mother home some hours ago. Barry had gone as well, pressing Domini's hands between his as he had done long ago when they had parted on the beach at Knightley . . . for good, they both knew that now.

Domini drew her coat about her and walked carefully to the door, for she didn't wish to wake Kara. She opened the door with equal care and stepped outside into a cool, antiseptic corridor, where already there was a busy coming and going of nursing staff and orderlies. Several of them glanced at her, but they seemed too busy to speak and she made her way undeterred to the floor on which Paul's room was situated. Arriving at the door, she hesitated, then eased the door open and took a look inside . . . Paul's bed was empty, the covers drawn aside, leaving a gaping, empty mattress.

Domini had never felt so cold, so acute a sense of loneliness as she stood looking at that empty bed. The indentation of Paul's head was still visible in the pillow, his wristwatch lay on the bedside table, the strap still curled to the shape of his wrist . . .

"Steady!" Firm hands took hold of her and impelled her into the room to a chair. She sat shivering while Dr. Suiza poured cold water into a glass and held it to her lips.

"You foolish child, to give yourself such a fright!" He spoke gruffly. "You should have waited for me to come and tell you that Paul has been taken to the operating theatre. His surgeon arrived half an hour ago."

The water was cold on her lips, the news a warm relief. "How long will the operation take?" she asked.

"Some hours, I am afraid. Look, child, why don't you go home? You are worn out already, and this hospital atmosphere will play more and more on your nerves as the hours go by."

"I'd prefer to stay," she said quietly. "I promise to be good. Kara and I will have some coffee from the canteen, then we'll wait on a bench in the grounds."

"As your doctor I should order you to go home." Metros shook his head at her. "But no doubt you would worry even more, waiting there for news. Very well, sit in the grounds. The sun is rising and it grows warm; you and the little sister will come to no harm there."

"The surgeon is good, Metros?" She sat looking up at him, with eyes too large in her pale face.

"One of the very best," he assured her. "He is tough and ruthless as Paul himself—and such men have their way, do they not?"

"Not quite—this time." She bit down on her lip. "Paul is sure to hate me when it is all over—but how could I let him die?"

Metros could still hear her saying the words, so simply, so quietly, as she walked away from him, along the corridor and down the stairs that led to the room where Kara might have awakened to find herself alone. Domini quickened her pace, eager to share with Kara the news that Paul was now in the hands of the surgeon, and the hope that his skill would give Paul his sight as well as his life.

The time passed slowly, and yet all at once it was over as Domini saw a nurse approaching the bench on which she sat with Kara. They rose and went to meet the nurse. Monsieur Stephanos was now out of the theatre, and they could come to the recovery-room just to have a look at him.

The nurse added — speaking in Greek which Kara translated — that the surgeon would then like a few words with Madame Stephanos.

Domini's heart gave a cold little jerk. She met Kara's eyes, appealingly, and Kara questioned the nurse in rapid Greek. "She says it is a formality," Kara said, but their fingers clung as they walked along the path between a double row of heart's-ease, and in under the shade of a side entrance.

CHAPTER FIFTEEN

PAUL looked as people always do after an exhausting and protracted operation, as though he would never wake again. His head was swathed in white bandages, and the quietness of the recovery-room was broken as Kara gave way at last and began to cry.

"I-it is because I am so happy," she sobbed. "S-so happy that Paul is g-going to get well."

The surgeon was a tall, blackbrowed man with heavy shoulders and an uncompromising manner. Madame must understand, he said, that it could not be certain at this stage whether her husband's blindness would be total or partial. In the course of extracting the metal splinter, the optic nerves had suffered damage . . . in short, Madame Stephanos must be prepared for the worst and hopeful of the best.

At best, it seemed, Paul would have the sight of his left eye.

Aunt Sophula insisted that Domini spend the next week or so at her house. It was closer to the hosptal; besides it would do Domini no good to worry alone in that big, empty house on the eagle's crag. Domini fell in with the suggestion, but she had to go home for some clothes, and she also wanted to assure Yannis and Lita that Paul was going to get well.

How quiet the house was, though far down on the beach men were moving to and fro like worker-ants. Some of them were blocking in the cave-tunnel which was no longer safe for use. Others were busy erecting an electric cable on which a cabin would travel up and down from the beach to the headland — Paul's idea, which had gone into operation some days ago. It would be very useful now, Domini thought. Paul would not run like a ram down the uneven-stepped path for many weeks. Maybe never, if the miracle she was praying for did not occur.

She wrote a long letter to her uncle before Yannis drove her to the old harbour mansion, sitting at Paul's desk in his private den, using the ornate pen that had belonged to his grandfather. There was a lot to tell Uncle Martin, but she didn't want to worry him too much and she made no mention of the baby she had lost. The letter ran to several sheets and it helped to put into words some of the deep anxiety she was feeling in connection with Paul. At last she laid down the pen and sealed the letter into an envelope, adding a Greek stamp and visualising her uncle as he opened the letter at the breakfast table in the shabby morning-room at Fairdane.

Fairdane seemed a long way away, a house in a dream where like Alice she had wandered and played and never quite grown-up.

She sat on quietly at Paul's desk, fingering the carving of the age-polished wood, and finally taking into her hand the little brass unicorn which she had given to Paul that honeymoon day in Looe. Strange, fateful day, the fabric of their night sewn happiness doomed to be torn into shreds before the sun went into the sea.

She traced with a finger the outlines of the unicorn . . . symbolic of the most elusive thing in the world, Paul had said. Symbolic of happiness; fabric of dreams, gift of the gods. She rose and made her way out of the den, carrying the unicorn like a talisman.

Lita had packed a suitcase for Domini and she carried it down to the front door for her. The door was open and a cluster of people waited on the steps, anxious-eyed, eager to hear from Domini herself that her husband was going to recover from his illness and be well and strong again. All of them had gifts of fruit and flowers for her to take to him, and as Domini's arms filled with the flowers she couldn't speak for the band of pain tightening around her throat. Tears gathered in her eyes, falling on to the lovely, scented mass of flowers as she buried her face in them and ran to the car.

The women in the crowd nodded to each other. The little Anglitha was touched by their gifts . . . such a nice girl for a foreigner . . . so much in love with her husband.

The next few days were made much easier for Domini by the company of Kara, and Nikos when he was home from work. He had a very serious and grown-up air since finding himself in full charge of the local office. "My son is almost a man," Aunt Sophula sighed over her lacework, as mothers will when they see the last traces of boyhood fading from the faces of their sons. "It seems only a day or so ago that I held in my arms a baby . . . ah, but forgive me, Domini, I should not talk to you of babies just yet. Though I don't doubt there will be others, with Paul making such progress after his operation. It will not be long now, child, before he is home."

Domini kept her eyes glued to the magazine she was looking at, for her conversations with Paul at his bedside had not included any mention of the future and what it might or might not hold. Kara always went with her on her visits and whenever she mentioned leaving them alone for a private chat, panic seemed to clutch at Domini and she was always glad to see Paul smile rather narrowly and order his sister to stay just where she was. Kara, looking like an elf in her best green dress, would curl down again on the side of his bed and shoot puzzled glances from him to Domini.

Domini saw those glances, though she pretended not to. She strove for as normal a manner as possible as the days passed and Paul's head-swathings grew less and less. Soon the bandages would be removed from his eyes. Soon they would know whether he was to see a little or not at all.

Domini was dressed to go to the hospital on Friday afternoon, when she discovered that Kara was nowhere in the house. Aunt Sophula couldn't say where she was, and she added that Domini should not hang about waiting for her. She was wasting valuable minutes of the visiting hour. "Will you come with me, Aunt Sophula?" Domini's fingernails bit into the raffia bag that held fruit for Paul.

"My dear child," Aunt Sophula patted her arm, "this is a golden opportunity for you to be alone with Paul. You should not be so good as to take Kara with you every time. I am sure she monopolises all the conversation. Such a chatterbox! She quite tries my poor old head at times."

"Paul enjoys the company," Domini insisted. "Please come."

It was then that Aunt Sophula looked at her very shrewdly. "Are you afraid to be alone with him?" she asked point-blank. "Do you fear he will blame you if when the bandages come off he is found to be blind?"

Domini went very white as she stood there in the cool hall of the house, wearing a blue suit piped with white: tiny lapis lazuli hearts clipped to her earlobes.

"Paul hated the thought of being blind, and dependent," she said. "I may have condemned him to that for the rest of his life."

"He has his life, has he not?" Aunt Sophula propelled Domini to the door. "The car is waiting, and time is going. *Adio,* my child."

"Aunt Sophula," Domini gave a tormented laugh, "you are ruthless."

"It runs in the family," the old lady said dryly, standing on the steps and waving as her chauffeur started up the old-fashioned car and it moved off sedately with Domini sitting tensely on the back seat.

Paul knew at once that she had come alone, and she talked nervously all the time she took grapes and peaches out of her bag and arranged them in the bowl on his bedside table. Petals were falling from the flowers she had brought the other day and she picked them up, crushing them in her hand as she turned to see him unrelaxed against his pillows, his mouth set in a stern line below his arrogant blade of a nose.

"I know you like seeing Kara, but—" There she broke off, too late to mind her words. "W-would you like a peach?" she stumbled. "I'll peel you one."

"Domini," he said quietly, "there is something I would like."

"What is it, Paul?" She stepped eagerly to his bedside. "Please tell me."

He turned his head and seemed to be looking right at her through the bandages. "I would like you to buy a plane ticket and go home to England," he said.

"What?" She stared down at him, unbelievingly.

"You heard me." He folded his hands behind his head, proud and dark against his white pillows. There were Venetian blinds at the windows and they cast tiger-stripes across his bed, one a bar of gold right across his brown throat where the jacket of his pyjamas lay open. Domini stared at his throat, and she saw it move as he swallowed.

"If you imagine I'm going to buy that ticket, then you're very much mistaken," she burst out. "I'm staying right here."

"They will turn you out in fifty minutes' time," he said dryly.

"Paul," she leant over him, supporting herself with one hand on the bed rail, her eardrops swinging against her cheeks, "I *had* to sign that form."

"You mean—they made you?"

"No—I did it for your sake. Darling—"

"What did you call me?" Again those lifted, bandaged eyes seemed to dwell on her face, and his mouth looked uncertain, relaxed from the sternness of a minute ago.

"I called you an arrogant Greek," Domini stormed. "Telling me to go to England! Do you think I'd go, with you like this? I've as much right to know whether that left eye is undamaged as you have!"

"Since when?" he demanded.

"Since you marched into my life and made me your wife!"

"Domini," his hand was searching and she put hers into it. His fingers closed tightly about hers, punishing and wonderful. "Are you sorry for me?" he asked.

"Sorry for you?" she scoffed. "I'm sorry for myself because I've got to put up with you for the next fifty years. Arrogant, bossy, master in your Greek house on the crag. What a life it will be!"

"I am not asking you to stay." His fingers unclosed about hers a fraction.

"You didn't ask me to love you," she said deliberately. "You told me to keep it. I'll keep it to myself if that's what you still want, Paul. I won't even stay for always, if you don't want me to, but for a while you're going to need me, and I'm available."

Then she gave a gasp as his fingers crushed hers again and he drew her hand to his lips. "How feminine to threaten and weep at the same time," he said against her fingers.

"I-I'm not—"

"Not feminine?" he mocked.

"Not w-weeping, you brute." She fell to the bed, buried her face in his shoulder and gave way at last to the stored-up tears. "My Samson, you really brought down the pillars this time," she said at last, wiping her cheeks on his pyjama jacket.

He gathered her close to him. "Sun, moon and stars are dark right now, Domini, as in Samson's song," he murmured. "What if they stay dark for me?"

"Two people can see across mountains and oceans, Paul, if they're together and in need of each other." She kissed him in the hollow under his cheekbone. "You feel a bit smoother now, darling. You looked awful just after the operation, all blue-jawed and piratical."

"Did I frighten you?" He stroked her hair.

"Has there ever been a time when you haven't?" she laughed.

His arms grew fierce, his lips were buried in her hair. "Beyond everything I had to have you, Domini," he said thickly. "There was no room in what I felt for compassion, for you or for myself. Do you understand?"

"I'm beginning to, at long last." Her teeth nipped his earlobe in loving punishment. "Making me your Sabine!"

"Now my Delilah, it looks like."

"It may never come to that, my darling," she said gently, and as he laid his face against her heart, her hand dwelt with compassion at the back of his head. "Dr. Suiza is very hopeful — we all are. Aren't you, yourself?"

"Do I deserve to be?" His head moved restlessly against her. "I took you away from all that was dear to you, tricked you that first night, gave you the heartache of a lost child—"

188

"Don't, Paul!" She pressed her mouth against his, warmly, persuasively, forgiving everything with a kiss as women have always done. "I love you," she said softly. "You made me love you a long time ago, but pride was always my sin and I wouldn't admit that love to myself, let alone to you. Oh, Paul, when they told me you were dying I wanted to die with you. Then when Dr. Suiza said there *was* a chance—a blind and terrible chance— I had to let you have it.

"Darling—Tiger—" She caressed the nape of his neck, the hard shoulders, her bones gone to honey as his arms reduced her to helplessness in the old way, her lips crushed, silenced, possessed under the mouth that whispered warmly—after a long while:

"I have had enough of this hospital. Soon they must take off these bandages, Domini, for I want to go home with you."

And not many days later they went home, where on the *piazza* of their sea-crag home, Paul wrapped an arm about Domini's waist and saw again the deep blue of the Ionian reflected in the eyes raised in love to his face.

It didn't show, she thought compassionately, that Paul was totally blind in the right eye. But each day the left one grew stronger, brighter.

Tiger-eyes, tawny and exciting as the dark line of his profile and the arm that bound her so close to him.

I love him so much, she thought wonderingly. Paul . . . dear, dominant Paul, who had faced the rage of guns and grenades at sixteen; whose sons would be equally bold and daring.

"We will make a good life together, eh, Domini?" he said. "Now it will be again as it was that day we were together in Cornwall. Do you remember the little unicorn?"

189

She nodded happily. "That little unicorn was in my handbag each day I came to visit you in hospital. He brought us luck, and happiness, Paul."

"And you brought me love," he added, taking her close and kissing her deeply, endlessly, until Yannis came out smilingly to tell them that tea awaited them in the *salotto*.

For more than 25 years,
Harlequin has been
publishing the very best
in romantic fiction.

Today, Harlequin Books
are the world's best
selling paperback
romances.

What the press says about Harlequin Books

"...clean, wholesome fiction...always with an upbeat, happy ending."
— San Francisco Chronicle

"...a work of art."
— The Globe & Mail, Toronto

"Nothing quite like it has happened since *Gone With the Wind*..."
— Los Angeles Times

"...among the top ten..."
— International Herald-Tribune, Paris

"Women have come to trust these clean, easy-to-read love stories about contemporary people, set in exciting foreign places."
— Best Sellers, New York